Praise for *A New Day*

"A wise and tender portrait of chance encounters and missed connections, Sue Mell's *A New Day* is a love letter to the people we meet along the way and those we leave behind. I loved it."

—Daisy Alpert Florin, author of *My Last Innocent Year*

"Sex, money, ambition, friendship; the myriad challenges of ordinary survival in *A New Day* are handled with wry and artful insight. Beautifully complex characters are pieces of a puzzle in this fine collection, while each story is both distinct and part of the whole."

—Louise Marburg, author of *You Have Reached Your Destination*

"An enthralling and visceral collection about both our inescapable interconnectedness and loneliness, the role chance plays in the decisions we make, and how even the most seemingly small moments irrevocably impact our lives."

—Ronit Plank, author of *Home Is a Made-Up Place*

"Clear prose, vivid scenes, and snappy dialogue bring Mell's well-developed characters to life. These linked stories explore relationships—evocative snapshots revealing desire, love, loss, and everything in between."

—Corie Adjmi, author of *Life and Other Shortcomings*

Praise for Sue Mell's *Provenance*

"If you've ever suffered a loss, if you've ever had to start over, you will find kinship and hope and even joy in *Provenance*, the story of a widower seeking to salvage his life after moving back to his small hometown in upstate New York. I cannot recall reading a debut novel imbued with such depth of understanding and compassion for its characters, or one that better captures the messy business of living. Sue Mell writes like a dream."

—Will Allison, author of *What You Have Left* and *Long Drive Home*

"A carefully crafted, impressively intriguing, and fully engaging contemporary novel that will have a special appeal to readers interested in family life fiction, *Provenance*, by the gifted author Sue Mell, is especially and unreservedly recommended."

—*Midwest Book Review*

A NEW DAY

A NEW DAY

STORIES

Sue Mell

SHE WRITES PRESS

Published 2024
Printed in the United States of America
Print ISBN: 978-1-64742-742-9
E-ISBN: 978-1-64742-743-6
Library of Congress Control Number: 2024904176

For information, address:
She Writes Press
1569 Solano Ave #546
Berkeley, CA 94707

Interior Design by Kiran Spees

She Writes Press is a division of SparkPoint Studio, LLC.

Grateful acknowledgment is made to the publications in which versions of the following stories originally appeared: "Serendipity," "House-sitting," "Single Lens Reflex," "Fallout," and "Lapses," in *Narrative Magazine*, "As If" in *JMWW*, and "Chances Are" in *Conversations: an Anthology* from Unleash Press.

CONTENTS

PART ONE
RACHEL

SERENDIPITY | 1985

Just because Rachel had been thinking she might run into Richard didn't mean she'd made it happen. Manhattan was a small town if you bought your gesso at Pearl Paint or had a fondness for the pignoli cookies at Rocco's Pastry Shop, or if next week, once your nearly perfect boyfriend had squared away the sublet, you'd be living within spitting distance of your old flame. Or whatever he was to her—never acting on their attraction having only elevated it to an even purer form of romanticized drivel. An obsessive yearning it had taken her years—and meeting Evan—to put aside. Still. Coming up from the subway at Christopher Street that afternoon, she'd literally crossed his path. Richard had grinned, linked arms with her, and swept her along down Seventh Avenue. Now here they were at the White Horse Tavern having a beer, and Rachel couldn't dispel the feeling that she'd conjured him up.

Richard was a painter and had been a visiting artist at NYU when Rachel was floundering her senior year. The first time they'd spoken, outside his class, had been the same day he'd begun his affair with another student, Ellen, the redheaded sculptor he still lived with, although—pretentious as ever—she called herself Lena now. That day, dressed in his requisite denim jacket and chunky black work boots, Richard had been looking for Ellen when he wandered into the atrium where Rachel stood despairing before a twelve-foot canvas taped to the wall, the backdrop she'd promised to paint for a parody of Chekhov. A whimsical Russian cityscape meant to contrast the dreary lives of sad, trapped characters with no chance in hell of ever getting what they wanted. She'd drawn a loose pencil sketch, even laid in some tones for the onion domes of Saint Basil's Cathedral before becoming paralyzed by the massive reality of the piece. There wasn't enough time to finish before opening night—let alone paint something good—and Rachel was less than thrilled to have Richard discover her, paintbrush in hand, frozen by the vast white wall of her impending failure.

"Stuck?" he asked.

"Little bit," she said, hoping he'd take her sarcasm as his cue to leave.

"None of my business, huh?"

Richard rocked on his heels but made no motion to go. Rachel laughed and threw up her hands. He came around and stood behind her, examining the problem from her point of view.

"Mickey Mouse," he said.

"*Excuse me?*"

"Mickey Mouse. It's a satire, right? Just treat it like a giant cartoon. Paint in all the outlines first—then you'll be able to see where you are, and fill in the rest. It's an old sign painters' trick, brought to you courtesy of an old sign painter," Richard said with a flourish of his hand. "Your sketch is nice—makes me think of those cityscapes by Stuart Davis."

Rachel told him she didn't usually look to Walt Disney as her go-to guy but that she'd give it the old sign painters' try. "Stuart Davis," she said. "Did you mean that? I love his work."

* *

Rachel had taken Richard's advice, and the painting had come to life—a playful jumble of bright-colored buildings with monuments of horses that seemed to fly through the air; it still gave her a kick to think of it. At the cast party opening night, Richard had been there with congratulations. Dancing with Ellen, he'd caught Rachel's eye and held her gaze, a look that said if she'd been there first, things might've been different. Rachel had smiled and waved him off; he was her teacher and now a friend—that was more important. Ellen might have great tits, but her sculpture was crap. As the year went by, though, that hadn't proved to be much consolation. Richard remained a champion of Rachel's work, and as the scope of her paintings grew, so did Rachel's attachment. As much as she tried to deny it, she wanted something more.

There'd been a time, those first years after college, when she'd looked for him everywhere. The determined hunch of his forward motion as he strode through lower Manhattan, sometimes up to Central Park. Richard's pulse was a sonar that would blip on her screen if she could settle down deep enough into an internal tracking that overrode the statistics of chance—it was mostly wishful thinking, but sometimes she could find him. Those meetings consisted of pointless cups of coffee, coinciding errands that filled Rachel with joy regardless, their connection reconfirmed. She'd always imagined there'd be some tertiary spin, like in a color wheel, where their shades would blend.

Then finally there'd been Evan, wispy blond hair forever falling into hangdog pale blue eyes. Goofy but solid, and smarter than anyone she'd ever met. Back then, he'd still been in law school, and he'd had to practically hit Rachel over the head before she took notice of him. He'd been a friend of her then roommate Colleen's, another redhead—she was surrounded by them! As the story went, he'd once asked her out, but Colleen had claimed she couldn't see him as anything more than a little brother, although they hung out constantly, which meant the three of them often did things together: double features, concerts at Hurrah or the Palladium. Sometimes Evan and Colleen came by the Upper West Side restaurant where Rachel was waiting tables, toward the end of her shift. They'd sit at the counter drinking milkshakes until she was done, and then Evan would walk the two of them home. It was like having a family, made her feel loved despite what she'd viewed as her hopelessly single status.

Once Evan had dropped by unannounced when Rachel was about to do laundry. She'd opened the door to his reliable smile with a basket of dirty clothes in her arms.

"Oh!" she'd said. "You just missed her! She went to grab a bite at that Greek diner—the one on Eighty-Sixth."

"Want some company doing laundry? I hear there are rats down there."

"Rat—singular, not plural—and I heard that the super put out traps. Why do you even know about that? Anyway, don't be silly." She'd locked the door behind her and pressed the button for the elevator. "Come on. I'll ride down with you," she'd said. "If you hurry, I'm sure you can catch her." It was a wonder Evan hadn't given up.

Months later, they were all at the apartment, and Evan was teasing Colleen for having no one besides a couple of Jews to help her decorate her Christmas tree.

"But I love Christmas!" Colleen said. "And you guys are my best friends." She was trying surreptitiously to thin out the strands of tinsel where they'd piled on too much for her exacting taste. Rachel and Evan were sitting on either end of the couch with their legs stretched out, but Colleen couldn't stop fussing with the tree. Every time she moved an ornament, Evan tapped Rachel's knee with his sock-clad foot, making Colleen's compulsiveness their inside joke. *I live with her*, she'd mouthed, and they'd both cracked up.

"Step away from the tinsel," Evan said, and Colleen, taking in the two of them, had stuck out her tongue.

"All right, all right," Colleen said. "I'm going to bed. Some of us have to work in the morning. Evan—you taking off?"

He glanced at Rachel. "In a little bit."

"Well, don't forget to unplug the tree, Rach. Okay? Those bubble lights are hard to find; I don't want to burn them out."

After Colleen had gone to bed, Rachel and Evan remained in the tree's blinking glow, reminiscing about the Hollywood-themed party the three of them had thrown for Halloween. Rachel had covered the living room walls with a roll of newsprint, and using a colorful array of magic markers, she'd drawn in Grauman's Chinese, the Hollywood Sign, and floor-to-ceiling palm trees. The final effect bringing to mind one of her favorite children's book illustrations: the unoccupied apartment painted into a jungle by the havoc-wreaking Curious George.

Evan had deejayed, mixing Squeeze with Stray Cats, Michael Jackson's "Thriller" into Deborah Harry singing "Heart of Glass." Colleen had taken care of the food and drinks, had sewn herself a replica of Dorothy's gingham pinafore from *The Wizard of Oz*, and using burlap and blue-gray felt she'd outfitted Evan as her Scarecrow companion. She'd captured all the details of the costume: the bits of loose straw, the rope ties and torn patches, down to the greasy brown triangle of makeup on Ray Bolger's nose.

"That was generous," Rachel said. "Letting her dress you up like that."

Evan turned to look at Colleen's tree. "She's been a good friend. And I think she's always been a little sweet on me."

Rachel laughed.

"Why's that funny?"

"Because that isn't . . . well, let's just say, that's not the way she tells it."

By the time Evan kissed her, the stars had spun across the sky, and the night was shifting from black to a watery blue. A crimson line lay across the horizon, and as the delicate hues of dawn spread across the room, Rachel rested comfortably in his arms, feeling both heavy with lack of sleep and elated that her life had changed when she'd least expected it. Like Dorothy in Kansas, she needn't have looked any farther than her own backyard.

"I should go," Evan whispered into her ear, shattering her reverie.

"*Now?*" she said. That was it? Just some holiday making-out spurred on by twinkling lights?

"I think I should tell Colleen first, rather than . . . us"—he gestured vaguely at the room—"here on the couch with her perfect tree . . ." He untwined himself from her, reached for the sneakers he insisted on wearing in every kind of weather. His use of *us* restored her calm—the guy was like some kind of a saint—of course they should tell Colleen first, but it certainly hadn't been on her mind.

"Shit," Rachel muttered as Evan stood up.

"Don't worry, she'll come around."

"No," she said. "It isn't that—I never unplugged the lights."

As she sat across from Richard in the dim barroom of the White Horse Tavern, it seemed to Rachel that some person was always standing between her and happiness. That year, as Christmas had come and gone, she'd waited impatiently for Evan to have his talk with Colleen. He'd finally taken her to dinner on New Year's Eve, and when Rachel met up with them at a party later, Colleen hugged her wildly at the door. Trapped in her arms, Rachel looked up at Evan, who tipped his hand back and forth: comme ci, comme ça. They'd counted down to midnight with Colleen and then tried to quietly slip away from the party. But Rachel's new navy wool coat, with her apartment keys, had disappeared. At the rumor of theft, everyone gathered in the host's bedroom. Rachel held up coat after coat from the heap on the bed until only one was left unclaimed. A peacoat, which Rachel granted was similar to hers, except for the cut of the collar and the set of keys that belonged to someone else—the addled reveler who'd evidently taken hers by mistake. In its place, Evan draped his beige corduroy coat over Rachel's shoulders.

"You're going?" Colleen said, her face crumpling into boozy tears of despair. "But you don't have keys!"

"It's okay," Rachel said. She took the tipping champagne flute from Colleen's hand, steered her from the bedroom to the less populated hallway, found her some paper cocktail napkins to wipe her eyes.

"I'm going to Evan's," Rachel said gently. "He was supposed to—I thought he told you. That you understood."

Colleen sniffled. "He did. I do. It's just . . ."

"Oh, honey, just what?"

"It's New Year's *Eve*," she sobbed. "And now it's the last time it'll ever be the three of us. We were—we were like—" Colleen blew her nose. "Like musketeers."

Rachel tried to feel only sympathy for her drunken friend, but a shiver of resentment ran through her. "We were," she said, holding Colleen close. "Just like musketeers."

Outside in the startling cold, Evan's coat felt more heavy than warm.

"That went well," he said. "Don't you think?"

She'd thrown her arms around him then, their laughter ringing out in the empty street.

Colleen, as Evan predicted, had come around, and since that inauspicious New Year's Eve, Rachel hadn't spent a night apart from him the past three years. They'd begun by staying over at each other's apartments, then sharing a room in the huge place up by Columbia he'd rented with two law students from his class. Now Evan was an assistant district attorney, and they were about to live together—just the two of them—for the first time. So what was she doing in a bar with Richard? Nothing, she was doing nothing wrong. And even if there was still a spark between them, that was not, as Evan would say, a convictable crime.

Richard in his same boots and jacket, smiling his same wistful smile, across the table. Had he ever tried to call or seek her out? No, of course he hadn't. He'd continued his life bound up with Ellen/Lena, featuring her and their minuscule apartment in his latest paintings. Content to leave his meetings with Rachel up to chance. Had she really expected more than his congratulations when she told him about Evan? Rachel raised her pilsner to her lips and tipped up the glass, but there was only foam left in the bottom. She signaled the waitress for their check.

Richard walked her back to Sheridan Square, neither of them speaking along the way. Stalled at the subway entrance, they forced commuters to veer around them. A warm breeze lifted Rachel's hair, the fall light fading and Hopperesque.

"Well," he said. "I guess that's it." As if it had always been Rachel's status that had tipped the equation.

"I guess it is."

Rachel loved Evan now—that wasn't the question—it was just that she'd always thought she'd been in love with Richard. Did moving in with Evan mean she no longer was? What about the feelings she'd had for Richard, all the yearning that had bored a hole where her heart should be? The red sign of Village Cigars across the avenue, the yellow taxis clogging up the crosswalk, for a moment these filled her vision like a glowing scrim. Richard said something, but his words merged with the sounds of the street.

"Wait," she said. "What did you say?"

Richard laughed and lightly touched her shoulder. "I said take it easy, kid."

"I will," she said. "You do the same."

Things were what they were, Rachel told herself as she skittered down the steps and pushed through the turnstile—it didn't matter. Except she knew that it did, that she wanted it to.

For the first three days she had the key to the sublet, Rachel carried it singly, in the front pocket of her jeans, separate from the ring of keys that belonged to more familiar doors. The fourth day she called information for Richard's number. He recognized her voice, wasn't surprised, though she'd never called before, said yes before Rachel could explain that she and Evan weren't actually moving into the sublet until the following week. Rachel understood the stakes had changed. Now that she also had something to lose, it amped the excitement, made Richard more willing to cross the line. It struck Rachel as odd that this was all it took, but she pushed the thought aside, let herself be guided by the ghost of desire she'd held for so long, her romantic notion of love, not calm and reassuring, but inescapable and true. He could meet her on Friday evening for a couple of hours.

Pleading girls' night out to Evan, her diaphragm already in place, Rachel boarded the number 1 train and rode downtown. As she was coming up the steps at Christopher Street once again, for just a split second the dark confused her; she'd somehow expected to walk back into the light of that last afternoon. Richard was waiting for her as planned, but instead of greeting her with the passionate embrace she'd pictured all the way down from 110th, he held down her wrists, keeping her firmly in place, arm's distance away.

"Are you sure you want to do this?" he said, his face contorted with concern.

"Are *you?*" She felt so keyed-up it was hard to breathe. "Jesus, Richard—you kind of scared me. We're not planning to *kill* anyone, are we?"

He snorted and let go. "I suppose not."

A gust of wind swept up litter from the curb, and Rachel swayed slightly, thinking of how easily she'd lied to Evan.

"C'mere." Richard pulled her toward him. "I just wanted you to be sure."

Standing stiffly in his arms, Rachel watched a bus speed down

Seventh Avenue. Then she buried her head in the soft worn fabric of his denim jacket. "Okay," she said. "I'm sure."

The apartment was just off the Hudson, a vague expanse of darkness whose smell could be rank but now carried only the faint salt-tinged scent of the ocean beyond. And despite the man-who-was-not-her-boyfriend she was bringing through the door, Rachel still felt the thrill of her new life on Morton Street, in the sublet Evan had secured for their future together. The lease belonged to his friend Eric, a lawyer moving in with his girlfriend in Chelsea, at her ultimatum. Of course he loved her, Eric had told them over gooey slices at a pizza place on Twenty-Third, but the apartment was subsidized—how could he just let it go? Rachel was the one who suggested he keep the lease and let them live there. Evan had been hesitant: there was a no-sublet clause, for one thing—not to mention almost tripling their rent—and hadn't they been pretty happy just where they were? Rachel had been stung by his lack of enthusiasm at the idea of them having a place by themselves. But then he'd surprised her by figuring out a way around the lease. They didn't need the second bedroom anyway; still furnished with Eric's things, it would remain an unused guest room, and given free rein to the rest of the place, "technically" they'd be his roommates and not his tenants.

Rachel's hands were shaking as she spread a clean blanket over Eric's gray cotton duvet. What would this little rendezvous be technically? Richard pressed his body into hers. He smelled of gesso and cigarettes, with a hint of almond from the artist's soap they both used to clean their brushes. He was already inside her, though they hadn't kissed, and just as her nerves began to ease, his fingers suddenly gripped her behind and he was done.

“Sorry,” he said, rolling off. “Kind of a lot of pressure.”

Rachel fully expected, once he caught his breath, it would be her turn, that they’d reconnect. But he only reached across her for his jacket, fumbling around in the pockets until he found his cigarettes.

“None of us smoke,” she said. “I wouldn’t want to arouse suspicion.”

“Right. Wasn’t thinking.” He asked if she was warm enough, covered each of them with the outside edges of the blanket. “This is a nice place,” he said, looking around the room. Then he began to tell her about his work and all the paintings he had yet to finish for a show in the spring. Too shocked to object, Rachel nodded along until it was time to go.

When she got home, Evan was still sitting up in bed with a legal pad, but instead of the appeal he’d been struggling with when she left, he was happily watching a basketball game on pirated ESPN. He’d been sketching the players and then crumpling up the yellow pages and tossing them into the small mesh wastebasket in the corner. Rachel picked one up off the floor that had missed the mark and smoothed out the paper.

“These are good, you know. You shouldn’t throw them away.”

“Nah,” said Evan, his focus on the game. “One artist between us is enough. Did you have a good time?”

“It was all right. Smoky bar. Think I’ll take a quick shower.”

She let the hot water run over her head, hoping to silence the barrage of thoughts rattling through her brain: You lie like a dog. You lie like a rug. *Out, out, damned spot.* Oh, great, Rachel—Shakespeare—very funny. *I am a seagull. No, that’s not it . . .*

“Okay, just stop it,” she said out loud, fiercely scrubbing her scalp with shampoo. Shakespeare wasn't bad enough—she was quoting Chekhov now? But the words persisted, and Rachel was surprised she still knew the lines: *Do you remember, you shot a seagull? A man came along by chance, saw it, and having nothing better to do, destroyed it . . .*

She leaned her head against the tile until the water ran cold.

The light was out, Evan asleep and breathing evenly by the time Rachel climbed into their bed wearing one of his sweatshirts. A drop of spermicidal gel trickled down her thigh. It was still too soon to take out her diaphragm safely. Carefully, Rachel backed herself into the warmth of his sleeping body. In an unconscious reflex, Evan wrapped his arm around her, filling her with grief.

The first time he'd told her he loved her—the first time he'd said it out loud—she told him she loved him too. Then he'd teased her mercilessly, saying: "*Love?* Who said anything about love? I said I *bug* you."

"I do," Rachel whispered in the dark, her throat constricting. "I bug you too."

Rachel busied herself with the move, setting up her workspace in the new apartment, replenishing her paint supplies at the pricier Flax instead of Pearl Paint, bypassing Christopher Street with the longer walks to the Sixth and Eighth Avenue lines—grateful for each day that passed between her and her careless transgression. Finding that the radiators at Morton Street gave off meager heat, Rachel splurged on a new down comforter, suggested they keep the door to Eric's room shut to avoid a draft. She studied Evan for signs of cognition, but he didn't seem to know anything had happened, and she slowly relaxed.

Christmas morning, Evan shook her gently awake, and Rachel became aware of a peculiar silence. This didn't bode well.

"What's going on?"

Evan slowly raised the blinds. Outside, the sun was shining and everything was buried underneath a pristine layer of crystalline snow.

"It's beautiful," she said, as though he'd given her a present.

"Well, you know. I do what I can."

Love and sorrow knotted up Rachel's heart.

"Better get dressed, pokey, we're already late."

"Oy." Colleen's holiday brunch. "White Christmas—how thrilled is she going to be?"

But it was Rachel whom the snow filled with joy, a clear and pure sign of a new beginning. She threw mittened handfuls of it into the air, laughed as the glittering particles fell all around her. They headed toward the subway at Christopher Street and, for the first time since they'd moved downtown, it was just a train station—nothing more.

"You're in good spirits," Evan said.

"It's Christmas! Fa-la-la-la-la!"

"Yeah, take it easy there, Santa," he said, steadying her on a patch of ice. "Let's not spend Christmas in the ER."

In the freezing station, there was only a homeless person huddled on a bench. Evan danced Rachel around the platform to keep her warm. She heard the singular clank of the track, felt the familiar faint rumbling beneath her feet. "Here comes our train."

"Not a moment too soon," Evan said, and kissed her.

Rachel ruffled his static-filled hair. Then behind him she saw

Richard and Lena come through the turnstile. Lena was stamping the snow off her boots, but Richard stared right at her.

"C'mon," she said, yanking Evan's arm as the train screeched into the station.

"C'mon, what?"

"The first car," she yelled. "We'll be closer when we get off."

"Okay, okay," he yelled back, laughing at her sudden desperation. "Whatever you want."

They raced through the doors of the first car just as they were closing. Evan slid into the orange seat beside Rachel and looked at her closely.

"Are you all right?"

"I am," she said, trying to catch her breath. "Just give me a second."

In a year, in another apartment, one with Evan's name on the lease, he would tell Rachel he wasn't in love with her anymore. He would swear there was no one else, but a few days later, when he was at work and Rachel returned to pack her things, a bit of trash in the mesh wastebasket would catch her eye: the empty box from a contraceptive sponge—who even used those anymore? She would come to think she'd made this happen after all, that her inherent ambivalence, albeit unspoken, had worn Evan down. And maybe there hadn't been anyone, anyone that mattered, until he'd ended it. But a woman had been waiting for her chance. Buying her lunch at the deli he favored for the crisp kosher pickles they tucked so neatly into the white butcher paper that wrapped their sandwiches. Lingering on the pillar-topped steps of the courthouse at Centre Street, feeling lucky to have landed a job in the same bureau of the trial division where

Evan worked, holding her breath each time the elevator stopped at his floor—his office a place Rachel had been too self-involved to ever go see. A woman she could easily imagine: always hoping for Evan, in his well-tailored suit, to come waltzing around her corner of the marble-floored hall.

LILY & DEVIN | 1988

The third time the waiter comes around with a pot of coffee, Lily places her hand over her cup—they should really get going, if they're going at all. Across the partition of condiments taking up half their table, Devin, the brooding, dark-haired man she's been living with for nearly a year, numbers apartments she's circled in the paper, creating a route of open houses within his price range. Having inherited some money from his uncle, he means to put a down payment on a two-bedroom, somewhere here in Brooklyn. Or so he says.

"I'll have a little more," Devin says to the waiter. "Then we'll take the check."

Devin hates his job, a well-paid position at his father's insurance company—one he swore through his pot-smoking twenties that he'd never take—and Lily knows better than to press him on his precious day off. In a few hours, she'll have to go into the city for her own job, leaving little time to find the rascal of their two cats. Marbella has wandered off for a day or two before, but the sidewalk's disappearing beneath a dusting of snow, and Lily's got a bad feeling.

"It's Sunday, Lil. If we have to hurry, I don't want to do this."

"I didn't say anything—what did I say? It's just . . ."

"Just *what?*"

"It's snowing, Devin, and she's out there—hurt or worse."

"Marbella?" he says, surprised.

"Yes—what'd you think?"

"I don't know, you're always . . ."

"Oh—*me*," says Lily, her fingers pressed to her chest. "*I'm* always."

"Let's just go." Devin works an arm into the sleeve of his peacoat. "I'll look for her—I promise." A smile flickers across his mouth. "While you're making the donuts."

It's a long-standing joke; Lily is an assistant pastry chef at the Plaza Hotel. But she's not in the mood and only zips up her parka.

"She's always found her way home before," he says, the words more critical than kind.

"And what if this time she doesn't?"

Lily met Devin at the Halloween party of a mutual friend. In a flowing white silk shirt and leather vest, a Guatemalan scarf wrapped around his forehead, he was a roguish pirate on his way out the door just as she arrived, wearing a fresh set of chef whites and a paper toque. They'd talked in the hall for what was left of the party, then gone out for pie at an all-night diner on Ninth Avenue. They dated a few months, then Lily had an ectopic pregnancy that cost her an ovary. She was living with a roommate in Brooklyn Heights, Devin had a tiny apartment in Jersey City, and the relationship might've gone either way. Up until then, she'd proved more sociable, wanting to attend parties together and engage with friends, to work toward building a life together; and Devin tended, more often than not, to act put out, dodging invitations and talk of the future. But after the hospital, after the surgery, he suggested Lily stay at his place, where he could take care of her till she got back on her feet.

A month went by, and then another, and then there seemed no reason they shouldn't go on. The place they rent now is in Fort Greene, and though it's a spacious ground-floor apartment with a private backyard, the neighborhood's still up-and-coming, their block sketchy at best. After Devin was held up at gunpoint walking home from the subway at DeKalb Avenue, even he had to admit the neighborhood was rough. The assumption is they'll keep living together, and, despite the skepticism of her friends, Lily clings to the idea that his buying a bigger apartment is a significant step—though he's yet to make an offer, snubbing place after place over a series of weekends.

The first two apartments they see that morning are a waste of time, but the third is stunning: newly refinished floors, Viking range, and a working fireplace in the living room.

The realtor is an overly tanned woman in her forties who keeps looking at her watch.

"The old cracked patio," she says of the pile of rubble taking up what, without it, would be a generous yard. "Demolition delays and blah, blah, blah, but the contractor swears he'll cart it all off next week. Some couples find that much lawn daunting. If it were me, I'd put in a deck."

Devin makes a face at Lily, as if to say, *Like anyone asked her.* In truth, there's no lawn to speak of, no bushes, no trees, and you can tell there's only bare dirt beneath the broken concrete and a thickening layer of snow. Landscaping, he's quick to point out, would be expensive. But Lily already pictures a raised bed of herbs and flowers, the delicate shade of an ornamental cherry, yellow rosebushes along the back fence. She drifts toward the empty fireplace, runs her hand across the mantle.

"It's a beautiful place . . ." the realtor says, her voice rising with the insinuation of other offers.

Lily glances at Devin.

"Yeah," he says. "I don't know—the living room seems a little *small*. Can you tell me the exact square footage?"

The realtor claps her hands together. "All in the specs. I left a set out on the kitchen counter."

Once Devin clears the room, she turns to Lily. "Usually the wives are the sticklers for details. How long you been married?"

Lily considers lying, then tells her they're not. "It's his money," she says, mocking the realtor's confidential tone. "He's really the one you should be kissing up to."

"I'll bear that in mind," the realtor says, each clicking step an additional rebuke as she crosses the room and vanishes into the kitchen.

Lily closes her eyes. It's the best place they've seen, but Devin still won't buy it—there's always going to be something that isn't right. She slides open the glass door leading into the yard, steps outside, and lets the cold air bite into her chest. She wants a family, doesn't want to return to her single life, to end up hunting for an apartment of her own. Something catches her eye—an orange tabby with a studded black collar slinking across the fence. The cat pauses to glare at her, then leaps into the adjoining yard. Lily glances back, makes sure neither Devin nor the realtor sees her, and doesn't bother to shut the door. She weaves around the rubble and unlatches the gate to the street, willing Marbella to be scratching at their own back door by the time she gets there.

In the first weeks after the ectopic, Lily took up knitting—a hobby she'd forgotten by the time she and Devin picked out two kittens at the ASPCA a few months later. Ruby, fluffier and silver-gray, grew into a docile, contented lap cat, a kitty-ecstasy of drool dripping from her mouth whenever anyone petted her. Whereas Marbella, with even her nose and the pads of her paws a tortoiseshell camouflage, barely tolerated any display of affection before wriggling free. Lily's friend Rachel—the only friend of hers Devin likes—does a fierce imitation of her quirky meow, a raspy, stuttering cry that sounds more like *M-m-meps*. Good kitty, bad kitty, Rachel predicted when, within days of their settling in Fort Greene, Marbella discovered Lily's bag of knitting buried among the boxes they'd yet to unpack, unraveled the cuff of a half-finished sweater, and nearly strangled her foolish kitten-self with the expensive yarn.

As Marbella grew, so did her repertoire of antics. She chewed on houseplants and dug up the tulip bulbs Lily planted in the yard; pawed furiously through the cat litter, then did her business just outside the box; tore through the house breaking table lamps and decorative objects. Their spring was punctuated by small crashes and continual trips to the corner bodega for overpriced tubes of Crazy Glue. By summer, Devin dubbed Marbella *Trouble*, and Rachel, maudlin and blue months after being dumped by her longtime boyfriend, had become an all-too-frequent houseguest.

One sweltering weekend, Lily made a strawberry-rhubarb pie, Devin barbecued, and Rachel, who'd brought the beers, drank a few too many, settling in for the night on the couch with Ruby. Lily and Devin were quietly making love when Rachel tapped on their bedroom door, complaining of a noise. Lily burst out laughing. Devin shushed her and held her tight, as though, if they didn't speak, she would go away.

"Not *that*," Rachel insisted. "A scuffle and a rattle—like someone breaking in."

"You girls," Devin whispered, his hand sweeping the floor till he found his jeans. "I'll go."

Lily pulled the sheet up to her chin, listened to their footsteps fade down the hall. Each night, when he came home from work, Devin dumped the coins and wadded bills from his pockets onto the faded blotter of an old oak rolltop desk in one corner of the living room—it still pleases her to live with a man who values that sort of antique. Half its pigeonholes are filled with business cards, receipts, and upcoming bills, but the rest contain mementos from years of travel. In one, a miniature brass Buddha sits atop a tattered map of Thailand. Another holds a string of chunky wooden beads, nickel *milagros* shaped like bent legs, and a set of tiny woven worry dolls nested in a bright yellow oval box. Items, like the scarf he'd worn the night they met, brought back from a Peace Corps stint in Guatemala. Yet another holds a broken piece of Moroccan tile and the saffron tin containing his stash—getting stoned a habit he hasn't relinquished.

Earlier that evening, before Rachel arrived, he'd asked Lily if she'd gone through his things, claiming there'd been a twenty among the crumpled bills—that it wasn't the first time some of his money had disappeared. She, in turn, had accused him of paranoia, suggesting he lay off the self-medication for a while, to which he'd snottily replied he didn't mind people *borrowing* things, as long as they *asked.* It had been a bad moment whose reverberating tensions—deferred by dinner and Rachel's presence—they'd just been smoothing out. As she waited for him to come back to bed, a breeze raised the sheers in a gauzy billow, and she sat up—no one was going to break in through the front door, but she put her hand on the phone just in case. Then light spilled into the hall, Devin's *What the fuck?* accompanied by Rachel's laughing *Oh, my God.* Lily flopped back onto the pillows, pulled the sheet up over her head, but Rachel wouldn't quit calling, saying she had to come see.

Resigned to more foolishness, Lily put on a robe. In the living room, Rachel and Devin stood before the closet, its door open wide. A pile of hats and gloves had been knocked to the floor, and in their place on the top shelf, beside Lily's rolling suitcase, crouched the cowering Marbella—a crumpled single clenched in her mouth.

"Aha!" Lily cried, coming up behind Devin and giving his shoulder a playful shove.

"Ow," he said, cradling his arm as though she'd actually hurt him.

Rachel looked back and forth between them. "What *ha?*"

"Nothing," Lily said, but Devin tugged on the belt of her robe, gently pulling her toward him.

"It's a little bit *ha*." He wrapped his arms around her, swung her slightly from side to side.

"Oh, now you think it's funny." She poked her elbow into his ribs. "Let go of me and help her down."

Unmoving, he looked at Rachel. "A scuffle and a rattle, huh?"

"Hey," she said. "Some of us were *sleeping.*"

Devin stepped toward the closet, but just as he reached up, Marbella leapt, clawing her way down the bare skin of his back. She thumped to the floor, scrambled through Lily's legs, and rebounded off the doorjamb, before skidding down the hall. They'd all laughed, and Devin even hugged Rachel goodnight. But back in bed, he complained about his scratches, and rather than help or comfort him, Lily told him where the peroxide was and turned away.

The subway platform at the Ninth Street station offers little shelter while Lily waits for the D train. Snow falls in a delicate curtain, sifting down through the tracks to the street below as garbled announcements broadcast borough-wide delays. When her train finally squeals into the station, it's already glutted with families dressed up for church. Lily squeezes on, is jostled to the center aisle, and barely manages to get off a few stops later. Ahead of her, a young Black woman in her Sunday finest tries to wrangle both a little boy and a baby in a stroller up the stairs to the street.

"You stop crying, now," the woman says, yanking the boy's arm, only making him cry harder.

From the crowd gathering at the bottom of the steps, someone chides the boy. "Hey. Little man. Why don't you help your momma?"

Lily looks back, connects the voice to a white guy in his thirties wearing a green combat jacket and a navy wool cap. *Why don't you*? she wants to say. Instead, she grabs the stroller's footrest and helps the woman up the stairs.

The wind has picked up, but the snow has stopped, and Lily exhorts herself to be grateful for this reprieve. In front of the bodega, a group of men pass around a forty. Shuffling and stamping their feet against the cold, they nod as she walks past. She's lived in this neighborhood long enough that most of the street hustlers leave her alone, but today of all days, a man calls after her, his steps closing in even as she picks up her pace.

"Miss, miss, hey, miss . . ."

Lily whirls around. "What do you want?"

"Nothing, *bitch*," says the wool-capped guy from the subway steps. "Your purse is open—thought you'd like to know."

Certain she's being set up, Lily holds his stare. Then she looks down. The clasp undone, her leather bag gapes open, its red lining torn.

"Oh, for fuck's sake." Lily digs through the bag, incredulous when she feels first her keys, and then her wallet, safely at the bottom. "How the hell? . . . I mean—thank you. Really," she says. "Sorry."

"Sorry?" He grins. "That all you got?"

Lily shakes her head, confused. She's already thanked him; what's she supposed to do? Get on her hands and knees?

"Found your wallet in there, dincha?" His voice a singsong now, his smile flirtatious. "How's about a little reward?"

If she told Devin about this—which she's not going to do—he'd dismiss her as careless and stupid. He could be so difficult—impossible, really—but then something would give, and what she thinks of as the real Devin, the man she loves, would reappear, making her dizzy with relief, then ashamed of her own impatience and doubt. This—some jerk hassling her for money—is what she gets for walking out.

Loose threads hang from the man's jacket where the name patch should be, his neck thick, his eyes bulging and bloodshot. He'd been right behind her in the station. Surely he'd opened her purse—her lurching forward with the stroller thwarting his theft.

"Are you kidding?" Lily says. "No—you know what? Fine." She digs back into her purse and pulls out her wallet. "Here's a dollar," she says, whipping out a bill. "Here's two dollars. You want three dollars? Oh, and look—here's a five-dollar bill." She turns the empty billfold so he can see. "That's all I got, okay? You want it? That's all I've got."

The man snatches the bills from her hand. "Christ, lady, you really *are* one sorry bitch." He turns toward the subway and walks away.

Lily just stands there shaking, her wallet in hand. Then she yells after him, "Yeah, you have a nice day!"

Determined to find Marbella, Lily bypasses their building and circles the block, peering into the yards and alleys, calling out her name. Rottweilers and Dobermans bark at her from behind windows and chain-link fences, but there's no bleating meow. Returning home, she holds her breath as she turns the key. If Devin was mad enough, he'd have taken a cab, gotten here before her. Inside, everything's exactly as they left it, and her bitterness falters at the sight of their intermingled belongings—even in this crappy neighborhood, they've made a beautiful home. Why can't that be enough? From her spot on the couch, Ruby yawns and blinks, then tucks her nose back into her paw. Lily lifts an old note from beneath a magnet on the fridge. It's a doodled drawing Devin made of the cats: Ruby curled up, asleep, in a flower bed; Marbella tiptoeing past, a tulip stem held in her mouth, the drooping blossom as big as her head. *Soon Spring*, the caption reads. How can she leave him? How can she go anywhere when Marbella is missing? She's going to be late for work, and any minute Devin's going to come through the door, her own vanishing act bound to win her the long-disputed title of Irrational One.

"Might as well live up to the hype," Lily says, patting Ruby on the head. After checking the backyard, she searches the house, looking in all the places she's looked before as well as those where Marbella couldn't possibly be. When she comes to the living room closet, Lily pulls her suitcase down from the shelf, a crumpled twenty flying out behind it. She picks up the bill, gathers the phone and its tangled black cord from Devin's desk, nudges Ruby over, and punches in Rachel's number.

"It's me," she says, when Rachel answers. "I might need to stay with you for a while."

"What do you mean?"

"What do I mean?"

"Don't get mad. I'm just asking how long. Are you leaving Devin?"

Ruby kneads her paws into Lily's hip. "Maybe. I don't know."

"Because moving in here—on a permanent basis? Maybe not the

best thing." Rachel's words rush out, as though she's been preparing for this. "Temporarily, *mi casa, su casa*, of course. But we're talking three cats in a one-bedroom apartment, and in the long run—"

"I should what, go fuck myself? You spend the summer moping on my couch—"

"*In the long run*," Rachel says. "I don't want us to break up."

It's nearly dark. A fumbling rattle of locks, the whining hinge as the front door opens and thuds shut.

"Well, look who's here," Devin says, sloughing off his coat as he enters the living room. He turns on the small ceramic lamp on the rolltop desk. Its pleated shade sits slightly askew; the crackle-glazed base has been reglued, but its harp is a little wonky from the last time Marbella knocked it over. "Don't you have to work?"

On the couch, Ruby is curled on Lily's lap, a wet patch of drool spreading across her thigh. "I called in sick."

Devin slaps down his keys, empties the bills and change from his pockets. "That's rich," he says. "How were those apartments, you ask? All those other apartments I gave up my Sunday to see, while you take off without—wait, you're sick?"

"Not that—don't be stupid. I'm fine." She's determined not to but begins to cry.

"What is it then?"

"I was getting my suitcase." She swipes away tears with the back of her fist and opens her fingers, the crumpled twenty in her palm.

Devin doesn't take the bill, doesn't ask why she was getting her suitcase. He sits down on the floor at her feet, rests his head against her knee. Ruby's tail flicks around his ear.

"Looks like Trouble's saving up for a rainy day," he says.

"Maybe we should get her a wallet."

"She can't have gotten very far without her cash."

"Oh, Dev," Lily says, breaking down. "I looked, but I couldn't find her."

"C'mon, Lilliputian, don't cry. I'll go with you. We'll look again." Devin presses his nose into Ruby's belly, gets up, gently lifts the cat, and resettles her on the cushion. "Up and at 'em," he says, nudging Lily's leg with his knee. "Chop, chop. Yo heave ho."

She tosses the twenty onto his desk and stands. They'll find Marbella, or they won't, and then what? She leans into him. "What's this? Role reversal Sunday?"

"Sunday's over, pretty much," he says. "But it isn't like you to give up."

The neighborhood's deserted and the temperature has dropped, snow glittering in windblown drifts beneath the streetlamps. Aside from calling for Marbella, neither of them speaks. Devin slips his hand into Lily's pocket, twines his fingers with hers. When they first moved to Brooklyn, they often took a Sunday morning stroll, Danish and café con leche in hand. An old brick church under restoration was a fixture of their route. Tattered plastic rattles against its scaffolding now, and a few browned stalks rise above the weedy churchyard where someone had optimistically sown a row of corn. Lily points to the sign with a painted thermometer depicting the congregation's funding goal, its red marker still stuck barely above the bulb.

"So much for revitalization," she says, but Devin shushes her.

"Listen," he says, and she hears it too—the faint, goat-like cry.

Wind whips Lily's ears, the sound bending around them, confusion spinning her in place. "Which way—which way? I can't tell."

Devin backtracks to the alley at the side of the church. "Over here."

Above cans of garbage and recycling is Marbella, caught between two bars of a wrought-iron gate, one back leg hanging limply behind her.

"Oh, Meps," Lily says. "Your leg."

"I'm pretty sure that's broken," Devin says. "Fucking Flying Wallenda." Together they compress the cat's limbs to thread her back out, then settle her in Lily's arms. "Flatbush," he says, and they hurry toward the wide avenue in search of a cab.

The price to set Marbella's leg—including kitty Valium, plaster cast, and the metal pins now securing her bones—is $2,700. That doesn't include the cab fare to the pet emergency hospital on the Upper East Side, where under harsh fluorescents the receptionist smiles up at them for payment.

Without looking at Devin, Lily reaches for her purse. "Half and half—split between our two cards—you can do that, right?"

"No," Devin says.

"No?" Lily's voice reels. "What no? You're not gonna chip in?"

He stares at her, reaching for his wallet, then shakes it in the air. "No, don't *split* it. I've got this, Lily—I've got the whole damn thing."

Devin's face is pallid and damp, his pupils contracted in the bright buzzing light. He taps his Visa card on the counter before them.

"Couple a thou?" he says. "Piece a cake."

The receptionist looks at her uncertainly.

"Devin," Lily says. "You don't have to do this—"

"I said I'd get it, okay? Try not to ruin the moment."

He slides his card toward the receptionist, who gives Lily a fleeting smile and picks it up. "They start out so cute as kittens," she says. "All at once? Or two installments?"

"All at once, please," he says. "I don't think I can take any more installments."

"I could throw in an Elizabethan collar," the receptionist says as she runs his card through. "Unless you already have one."

Devin turns to Lily.

"One of those cones," she says, fanning out her hands beneath her chin. "So she doesn't lick her wounds."

"Right," he says, signing the receipt. "Like that's going to stop her."

At home, Devin digs out the old cat bed neither animal took to, then he and Lily fall into their usual routine. She feeds the cats and begins making dinner from what's left in the fridge, and he clears the table of the Sunday *Times*, sets out cloth napkins and utensils. She slices up the tail end of a loaf of French bread, fits the pieces into the toaster.

"Ahh," says Devin. "What's better than the smell of toast?"

Lily adds butter to an enameled skillet, adjusts the flame. With one hand, she breaks eggs into a bowl. "I don't know. What?"

"No, I mean that smells good. Beer?"

"Sure," she says, whisking in milk, then a scattering of herbs.

Devin pours her beer into a Flintstones glass, takes a swig from his own, then leans against the counter watching her swirl batter around the pan, grate in Parmesan once the liquid is set, and dish the halves of a delicately folded omelet onto Fiesta plates. Devin has a dish or two he learned from his grandmother, but Lily's the cook of the house, a point for which—however teasing at times—he's always granted admiration.

After they've eaten, they ferry Marbella to the bedroom, set the cat bed down at the foot of their own. "*M-m-meps,*" she squeaks, a sound so strung-out and pathetic that they collapse, rolling on the floor in giddy laughter like a couple of kids up way past their bedtime.

"Poor baby," Lily says, pulling herself back together and scratching Marbella's neck beneath the cone.

Devin stands, brushes dust and fur from his jeans. "Well," he says, holding out his hand to help Lily up. "At least we know where she'll be."

They undress and climb into bed, take their positions for sleep. Lily on her stomach, one arm thrown around a pillow and one foot dangling off the mattress; Devin lying on his side, faced the other way, his fists tucked under his chin. Thinking she's heard his breathing level out into unconsciousness, Lily's surprised to hear him murmur her name. Rolling toward him, she leans up on one elbow, smooths her hand across the topography of his shoulders, Marbella's summer scratches long gone. Letting her fingers come to rest in the soft curve of his waist, she hears his breath catch with something more than her touch.

"That apartment," he says. "It was nice . . ."

Where the base of her thumb lies against his skin, Lily feels her pulse, the distant echo of her heart. "But you can't buy it."

"It's not . . . it's just . . ."

"You're not ready," she says. "I know."

"And that fucking suitcase—was that Rachel's idea? Because I—I don't want you to go."

Lily lets the weight of her torso sink back into the bed. In the silence that blooms between them, the siren of a police car rises and fades away. When Devin speaks again, his voice is strained and small.

"Can't we just stay here for a little while longer?"

Six weeks in the cast, the vet said—for the bone to knit back together, for new tissue to harden around the pins—and she'd be good as new. Lily is uncertain whether her answer, or even Devin's meager proposal, will hold. But she tips her forehead into the warmth of his back anyway.

"For a little while," she says. "Yes."

DECORATIVE ARTS | 1992

The streets in Bernal Heights were narrow, Rachel's building set into the crest of a steep incline, and in Paul's search for a spot to park, a succession of one-way streets funneled him right back down and around the way he'd come. Eventually, he found a space he could squeeze the truck into at the base of her block. He probably should've called. But she might've screened, and he might've left some ridiculous message she wouldn't bother to return. They couldn't seem to date, she'd once complained. Even the first time around, they'd begun in the middle somehow. "Instamacy," one of the counselors at Alta Mira called it—a kind of natural rapport that skips the usual hurdles of getting to know someone.

He'd left his house in Berkeley in denim overalls and a green pinstripe oxford. Clothes tidy enough, if not altogether clean, for the eight o'clock meeting on Bancroft, where he wouldn't run into Celeste, his now ex-girlfriend. After the meeting, he'd meant to swing by Home Depot for a bag of grout, to finally replace the crappy linoleum backsplash of his torn-up kitchen with half-inch tiles of aqua and blue, some of them faintly iridescent. Tiles whose varying shades recalled the slide sheets of swatches Rachel received from her rep, predicting the season's color trends. His thoughts often wound their way back to Rachel when things took a dive, as though she were an answer to a question he could never quite form, a place of comfort he could still return to, a puzzle he might finally solve.

They tried making a go of it every couple of years, as if by tacit agreement. One of them calling or showing up just when the other one needed. Each disastrous ending more than likely—though not entirely—his fault. Three weeks was about the longest they'd lasted. And yet their connection remained, like some uncashed check in a forsaken stack of bills. The sex hadn't been too shabby either. Blowing past the exit for Home Depot, he'd headed straight for the Bay Bridge. Surely enough time had gone by that she'd be glad to see him.

Rachel's apartment was the ground floor unit of a two-story building. A few carpeted interior steps led down to the glass-paneled front door, a venetian blind mostly obscuring any view inside. Broken across the panels, amid the cars and trees, was his own reflection: a broad-shouldered man in a Carhartt jacket layered with dabs of paint. Less heavy, he hoped, than the last time she'd seen him, but with the same messy peaked haircut, the same reddish mustache and short, boxed beard he'd been wearing for nearly twenty years. Not exactly rakish, but not displeasing either.

He rang the bell and waited, was about to ring again when he heard the thud of footsteps and caught a glimpse of men's cowboy boots through the loose bottom slats. The door opened on a man of Paul's height but of a wiry build. Skinny jeans and those slant-heeled boots, the toes well-worn and pointing upward, a vintage Hawaiian shirt loose on his taut frame.

"You're not the taxi," he said, then called back into the apartment, "Rachel, I think this is for you."

The man's face was craggy and yet pixie-like, his expression wry as he rested his hand against the doorjamb. Paul felt his measure taken. *Well, that's that,* he thought, Celeste's catchall phrase for when things didn't go her way. Two women now he'd need to get out of his head. "Guess I should've called."

“Never hurts. I’m Frank. Rachel’s an old friend of my wife’s.”

Before Paul could recalibrate or even give his name, Rachel’s voice proceeded her down the stairs.

“Less than fifteen minutes, the dispatcher said, and it’s already twenty-five. Who’s ringing the bell if it’s not the fucking cab?”

“It’s not like they’re going to start without us,” Frank said, quietly.

“Paul?”

Frank dropped his arm to make room for her in the doorway.

Rachel’s hair was cut short, and her neck, free of the tangle of light-brown curls Paul remembered, was startling in a way he couldn’t account for. He raised his hand and wriggled his fingers. “Long time no see.”

Rachel hesitated, her expression more stunned than amused. In a pair of sweats and an old tie-dyed T-shirt, she looked pale, her eyes red-rimmed.

“You’re not dressed,” said Frank.

Rachel looked at Paul and shook her head. “You ever think of calling?”

Frank said, “He was just regretting that. Is Lily all set? I’ll entertain your friend here for a minute. You’re going to at least want shoes. Tell her I’ll be up in a sec.”

“She doesn’t want me to come, okay?”

“Of course she does.”

“I believe her exact words were ‘You are not coming to the hospital.’”

Frank frowned. “I thought she just didn’t want you to drive.”

“That too.”

Both of them turned and looked up the stairwell. In place of the pregnant woman Paul expected to see, a thin woman in a pencil skirt stood poised above them, the stark navy and white stripes of her boat-necked sweater echoing the bands of light and shadow from the venetian blinds. With one hand on the banister, she seemed to waver. Her face an ashen oval, catching more and more of the light as she slowly stepped down, a carry-on suitcase thumping behind her. The dark circles under her eyes disappeared in the shift of rimless transitional lenses, and for an instant her expression held a chilling glamour, followed by a scowl as she squeezed past Frank and Rachel and spun the bag around on the sidewalk behind Paul.

"What are we doing? I thought the taxi was here. Do you have a to-go cup, Rach? God knows how long we'll be sitting around in registration. I'd like one last decent cup of tea. You going to introduce me to your friend?"

"Lily, Paul. Paul, Lily."

Lily studied him briefly and turned to Rachel. "Not Paul, that sculptor guy."

"The same," said Rachel, then to Paul: "And these are my people, from the land of tact. There's a couple of car cups in the cabinet above the sink. Now could we please stop acting like everything's just fine?"

Paul kept thinking there'd be an opportunity to extricate himself, to apologize for his timing, or at least ask Rachel what was going on, but the conversation leapt around him.

"This is exactly why I don't want you to come," said Lily. "Nothing's fine—you don't think I know that? But it's not happening to you, is it? And it's better—it's better for me—if I can keep it together. You can't help me do that? Spend some time with Cameron and look after Frank—is that so much to ask?"

"I should go," said Paul, and they all turned to look at him.

"Lily," said Frank. "It'll be all right."

"You don't know that," she said.

"Look," said Rachel. "Either take my car or I'll call another cab. But let's get out of the doorway."

Lily leaned into Frank, who put an arm around her shoulder and led her back inside.

Paul dug into his jacket pocket for his keys.

Rachel said, "Grab her suitcase, will you? You might as well come in too."

On the landing, fanned out around a striated industrial carpet of avocado green, the doors to the rest of the rooms in her apartment were shut, and while sunlight leaked into the stairwell, the foyer remained dim. Except for a corn plant nearly as tall as he was, the wide, high-ceilinged area was empty, which made him want to laugh. All that open space and nothing in it! Nothing but he and Rachel, looking like she'd just rolled out of bed. She turned to him now, and he felt a pleasant rush of anticipation.

She said, "This was Frank's idea—their staying here. That she'd have me to help take care of her. He doesn't understand that Lily can't bear it."

"She doesn't want to be taken care of?"

"Not by me. Lily has always been the stable one. Pisses her off to no end to have the situation reversed."

"So you and Frank, then—nothing going on there."

"Oh, my God. Is that the only way you can see things? Not everybody fucks everything else."

"Everyone, you mean."

"Isn't that what I said?"

"Everything, you said."

"And that's different how?"

At Paul's eye level, tips of several of the corn plant's variegated leaves had turned brown. Bending down to the planter, he felt dry dirt. "When's the last time you watered this?"

"So you just dropped by to check up on my houseplants? It's not good to overwater them. You can ask Frank—he used to have a plant store. That big palm tree in the living room? That used to be theirs."

Through the French doors, Paul could see a large suitcase open on the floor beside a palm tree whose uppermost fronds bent against the ceiling. "I did drive all the way across a bridge. That should count for something."

"Hang on. I've got a medal right here."

"Rachel."

"What."

"Let's go get a cup of coffee."

"Why? Do I look like I need one?"

"Yeah," said Paul. "You kinda do."

"I can't even remember the last time—" Rachel pressed a hand to her mouth. She shook her head and started to cry. "Sorry—just give me a second. It's not you—"

She leaned into him then, the same way Lily had leaned into Frank. Paul wrapped an arm around her, letting his hand rest lightly on her back. He was aware of the warmth of her body, that she wasn't wearing a bra, and that making a move would be wrong in any number of ways. He leaned back and bent his head down so he could look into her face. "Well, I'm glad we've established that."

"It's not funny—I'm a mess."

"No—you look . . ." He paused too long and she pulled away, using the sleeve of her shirt to wipe her face. The best he could do was try for a joke. "You could maybe use a new pair of pajamas."

"Okay, okay," she said. "I'm all right."

Rachel went into her bedroom, presumably to change, though he wasn't sure. He'd obviously shown up at a terrible time. Maybe he should go. Back to Berkeley. Back to his kitchen tiles.

"You can wait in the studio," she called out. "You don't have to stand in the hall."

Again, Paul noted the series of doors. *Like the lady or the tiger*, he thought to say but changed his mind.

The last time he was here, Rachel had just moved in, after a breakup of her own. Another illustrator—or had it been a cartoonist? Paul sat in the raised chair at her drawing table. One of those fancy rolling chairs with a metal ring to rest your feet on, levers to adjust the height and every possible angle of the back and seat. It huffed when he dropped it down. He'd been the one to suggest she use Celotex rather than the heavier sheets of Homasote she was going to hang as bulletin boards across the walls. Now nearly every inch of them was covered with reference and inspiration, the scraps and doodles that fueled her designs.

The last time he was here, he was still making stand-alone pieces of wooden furniture whose exaggerated shapes and extended surfaces created a canvas for his narrative designs. Raked angles framed curious interior spaces. The small door of a nightstand, set on spindly legs, might open to reveal the landscape of a wintry wood or a house going up in flames. The etched lines and painted details on a pair of side tables might map the memory of a city street or the scenes of a dream. Imagery spilling over edges and into drawers, as though still unfurling, a continuum of story and motif in motion across static form. His own studio, a converted garage behind the Craftsman house he'd inherited from his uncle—and done considerable damage to, during his cokehead days and the manic episode they'd triggered—was now padlocked shut, and the only work he'd done since getting clean was some custom carpentry.

Celeste, whom he'd met in NA, had encouraged him to build his own client base, to hire day laborers to help finish the repairs on the house. And yet he'd kept working as a day laborer himself, making kitchen cabinets for a contractor. Celeste was smart and thoughtful, and instead of not calling her for days at a time, he could've asked her to move in. Did she really mean to break up with him after nearly a year? Or had she just been asking for more of a commitment? They'd been apart now only a few weeks, and he wondered if she expected him to make a grand gesture. They weren't where they should be, was what she'd said. Maybe that was why he'd driven to Rachel's—because she'd known him when he still saw himself as a rising artist and not some cabinetmaker in recovery. Two years, almost to the day, since he'd gotten out of rehab. Two years since he'd made anything of his own. Even longer since he'd seen or spoken to Rachel. He both wanted and didn't want to tell her.

On Rachel's studio table were progressive jars of water, from murky to clear, and a series of fine-tipped sable brushes laid out on a clean fold of paper towel. Whatever else was going on, she was still working. There were small plastic palettes of gouache and several six-inch squares of teal paper with repeating patterns of tropical leaves and flowers painted in varying scales. Fabric design. That's what the color swatches had been for. Besides fabric, her whimsical work appeared on decorative napkins and paper cups and accompanied the articles in food and travel magazines. Illustration, she once told him, was keeping your hand in while doing someone else's bidding. A hundred things could disappoint, from cheap printing to last-minute cuts. But to have your images living out in the world was pure pleasure—more than perfection or fame. An addendum directed at his own obsessions.

"Paul," said Rachel from the doorway.

"Hey. What?"

"You messed with my chair?"

"No. Well, I lowered it, yeah. It's pretty comfortable. Is it ergonomic?"

"Not if you sit in it long enough."

He stood up, raised her chair to his approximation of where it had been. She'd put on a pair of jeans and a navy T-shirt with a bit of embroidery. A dashed line in shifting hues running along a V-shaped neckline. That sewn detail was about as feminine as Rachel would allow. Celeste had dressed up without occasion, in a layering of dresses and cardigans, scarves and vintage jackets, loose and tailored garments put together in a way that captured both a distinctively modern and a nostalgic, almost Edwardian, style. Just for the joy of it, she said. Seeing them together, people had often remarked that he was a lucky man.

"You look nice," said Paul. "You okay?"

"I must've told you about Lily and Frank. The restaurant closing? How they moved to DC?"

Paul shrugged with chagrin. He remembered she'd taken over the apartment from friends, but that was as far as it went.

Rachel frowned. "Anyway. This used to be their kid's—Cameron's—bedroom." She indicated the ceiling, where Paul could make out a constellation of glow-in-the-dark stars. "I could never bring myself to take them down. Cameron's an hour or so away, with an old friend of Frank's from culinary school. And Lily has . . . she's having a bone marrow transplant. That's what you walked into the middle of."

"That's gotta be tough."

Rachel came around the table, sat in her chair, and readjusted the height. "So what's happened to you then—someone dump you?"

Paul smiled, slightly stung. He hadn't quite thought this through.

"Right," she said. "I don't suppose it ever occurred to you that I might be seeing someone."

What he wanted most to do was sit down himself. "You know what would be good in here? Another chair."

Rachel took up the brushes and plunked them into a jar with ones of similar size. "I've been mostly preoccupied with other things."

"They're so intricate," Paul said, of the floral squares. "Very retro-Hawaiian."

"For women's bathing suits, okay? Don't get on my case."

That was what he'd done before—given her flak for doing work that was primarily commercial. He remembered a particularly sticky argument about greeting cards. "It just looks like you've been hunkering down."

Rachel nodded.

"So, you up for a cup of coffee with an old . . . ?" He didn't finish, and she didn't help him. "You're going to make me beg?"

Protecting each piece with a layer of tissue paper, Rachel gathered her designs into a single pile. "A cup of coffee," she said flatly, and he knew he'd pushed too hard. But then she looked up at him, her lips pursed to one side against a smile, and added, "would be good."

The coffee shop's storefront windows displayed a collection of antique tin toys arranged by category: cars and trucks, spaceships, human figures, and animals. The sort of flea market and thrift store finds whose particular palette had inspired his own work. Tomato soup red and yolky yellow, dense pistachio and limey greens, royal and cerulean blues, everything tinged with a dark undertone like forties newspaper comics. Paul took the toys as a sign, an indication of rightness, as he followed Rachel inside.

A pair of baristas was slowly replenishing plastic lids and stacks of paper cups bearing the shop's logo, a silhouette of a dapper man in top hat with a walking cane. Paul and Rachel had a mutual friend, James, who'd introduced them, Rachel having designed the confetti-like rain of coffee beans still being printed on the to-go cups of the Berkeley café James no longer owned.

"I haven't seen James in ages," Paul said. "You ever talk to him?"

She shook her head. "Not since he sold up. Lily always hated this place. 'Too many poseurs,' she said. And that the coffee was bitter—though I don't think that part's true."

One of the baristas had long black hair like Celeste's. A bracelet of hibiscus was tattooed around each of her wrists, her thin white arms emerging from a snug-fitting wife-beater dyed a crimson red and emblazoned with black painted letters that read Fuck Art. With a glance and a slight tip of his head, Paul drew Rachel's attention to the woman's top. "How do you think she means that?"

"Must be nice to be so oblivious," she said. "What do you think our chances are of ever getting any coffee?"

The other barista, a bleached blonde in a lacy camisole the peach color of a vintage slip, had a full set of tattoo sleeves—a twining array of birds, flowers, and skulls—and a voice that carried. "He calls me up Friday," she said, breaking down the empty carton from the cups, "at like eleven. Classic booty call, right? And I'm okay with that, because—you know—it's good. Really good. But then I don't hear from him. What is it now, Wednesday? Five days and nothing. Zip."

"Unbelievable," said Rachel.

But it wasn't the bad service that rattled Paul so much as the woman's mention of the day. Wednesday mornings Celeste led a meeting, for women only, at seven o'clock. There'd been no need for him to skulk over to Bancroft, no need to get in his car at all.

"Hello," Rachel said, in a futile attempt to get one of the baristas' attention.

"Five days and I'm thinking good riddance," said the one with black hair, now busily realigning the rows of cups. "Seriously. The guy's not invested—you should block his calls."

Rachel turned to him. "Why'd you come here today?"

He felt transparent. "What do you want me to say? For more than Mr. Calls Me Up Friday, okay?"

"Today, Paul—I was only asking why today. When you showed up, it seemed like—"

"All right," sighed the blonde barista, as though forced to make good on a wager she'd lost. "You two know what you want?"

Nerves buzzed in Paul's chest. "It seemed like what?"

"A latte," Rachel said.

"What were you going to say?"

"Nothing. You better order while you have the chance."

"Just a coffee."

"Five-fifty," said the barista, passing him an empty paper cup.

"Now she's in a hurry," Paul said.

The barista bristled, her hand in the air above the register. "Excuse me?"

"You don't have to do that," said Rachel, as he laid down the bills.

"What's a couple of bucks between friends?"

"No need to be rude," the barista muttered as she rang them up.

Looking for her commiseration, Paul turned to Rachel in annoyed disbelief, but she seemed to be considering the selection of pastries. "Did you want something else?"

"Lily wouldn't eat any breakfast," she said. "All she had was that stupid tea."

Before he could respond, she'd moved toward the door saying she'd grab a table outside.

Paul set their drinks down on the wobbly table she'd chosen beneath a bottle brush tree, the sidewalk strewn with its fallen red threads. Sweeping more strands off the vinyl seat of a bentwood chair, he said, "Exotic flora everywhere."

Rachel took a sip of her latte. "Hot. But good."

He sat facing the street, where the houses appeared to stack up in a panorama. A staggering of pastel gables flattened against the hillside, configurations of tiny black windows, each framed in white trim. Dark crowns of trees clustered against the sky, a scab of red cliff, the mossy green mesa. The stark shadows of a frieze. Just the sort of vista he'd once tried to capture the feel of in paint and wood. He took the lid off his coffee, let the steam rise up to his face. "I'm sorry about your friend."

"What I really feel like doing," she said, "is going to see the giraffes."

Unable to contain himself, Paul laughed. "That is possibly the saddest thing I've ever heard."

For a few seconds, Rachel just stared at him. Then she started laughing too. "It's so stupid, I know! The giraffes. Nobody goes to see the giraffes—I mean, kids do. Kids love the giraffes. Those patterns. And the way they lope—"

"Rachel. It's all right."

"If I stay home—"

"I get it. You'll just be thinking of your friends at the hospital." Paul stood up and held out his hand. "C'mon. We'll go to the zoo."

The sun was shining, the air was warm—he could think of worse ways to spend the afternoon.

Instead of the freeway, Paul took the side streets up and over Twin Peaks, resisting the urge to rest his hand on Rachel's thigh, as he'd done the first day they'd ever spent together. The hike he had planned at a state park in Marin was precluded by a sudden heavy rain, and he'd felt the capricious weather, the steady rhythm of the windshield wipers, binding them together. At each natural junction of parting, they opted to go on, afternoon merging into evening, a sushi dinner out, and then the night at his place. In the morning, he'd driven her home, the day sunny and startlingly clear. But then, one thing after another—he was preparing for his first show in L.A. and hadn't wanted to be obligated to anything but the work. Of course Rachel was working, too, though he hadn't seen those things as being of near, let alone equal, value. Not then.

"Go farther," she said as he began pulling into the first row of empty spots.

"Can't we enter here?"

"No. The main gate's more toward the middle."

"You're sure?"

"Is it gonna kill you to take my word? Oh, for fuck's sake." Rachel shook her head. "Why does that keep happening?"

Paul shifted into reverse. "What keeps happening?"

"Stop," she said. "Stop the car!"

He braked hard as a black Mercedes, not unlike Celeste's, passed directly behind them.

Rachel closed her eyes. "I'd just like to go five minutes without thinking—even tangentially—of somebody dying."

Paul drove farther into the lot, chose an oceanside spot just beyond the gate. He thought of Lily spinning her suitcase to a halt beside him. "Is that really a possibility?"

"You just nearly got us killed in the parking lot of the zoo."

He put the truck in park and waited.

"Fifty-fifty chance," Rachel said. "She wouldn't tell me, of course. But Frank did."

"I don't know what to say."

"Nothing to say. She's my oldest friend."

Beyond the Great Highway, waves cut diagonally across a shallow expanse of white and roiling water, and Paul couldn't tell whether the tide was coming in or going out. A tall wire fence and a short rise of oleander and beach grass separated the parking lot from the road, and he found himself staring at an inexplicable piece of architecture.

"What am I looking at?" he said.

"The ocean? Something beginning with the letter *B*?"

"No, no—right there—look at that. It's like a ruin."

"I haven't been here since Cameron was little," Rachel said, "but I don't remember seeing that before."

They got out of the truck and approached the fence. What must've once been the grand entrance to some sort of pavilion was now a freestanding facade of three doorways that no longer led anywhere. There was a carved medallion above each opening, a bas-relief column on either side, and a notched lintel that ran the length of the top as though holding the fragment together. Like a giant triptych, each doorway held its own brilliant abstract of texture and color. A layer of sand and scrubby grass, then a cropped segment of highway and a gray strip of ocean, then a block of blue sky. The face stood in shadow, but the left edge of the structure and the right side of each rectangular gap caught the sun in a pattern of radiance. Paul felt himself both lifted with pleasure and pulled down by a sense of loss.

"Random or deliberate?" Rachel asked.

"Does it have to be one or the other?"

A seagull passed overhead, its cry long and piercing, as they turned toward the zoo.

"It has to be something," she said. "I'm leaning toward random."

"Looks abandoned to me."

"So . . . what? They're loading up the flatbed with building parts and the foreman says, 'Screw it, we've got enough doorways'?"

"It could happen," said Paul. "One scenario."

"Oh, a scenario," Rachel said, drawing out the word. "Next thing you'll be telling me how much you've missed me."

"Did I mention I drove across a bridge?"

"Ah. Repetition. That is your signature move."

"I have missed you," he said, feeling truth in the words as they left his mouth.

"Yeah," Rachel said. "I'm sure."

The line at the gate was short but slow-moving. All moms and nannies with young kids, except for the huddle of teenagers that had gathered behind them. Two girls and a handful of boys—ditching tenth grade, was Paul's guess—reeking of pot and carrying on about the price of admission. Rachel glanced back, then gave Paul a small bemused smile and said, "Five dollars says they don't go in." When they got to the window, Paul tried to pay for them both, but she slid a twenty under the glass and told him not to be ridiculous.

The African section wasn't far from the entrance, but the herd animals—zebras, giraffes, and greater kudu, according to the plaque—were held in one large enclosure. Free to roam about, the giraffes were some distance away. Paul and Rachel followed a curving path through patches of sunlight and cool corridors of shadow formed by rustling eucalyptus and the arching branches of other trees he didn't recognize. They passed a netted aviary, whose shrieks and looping whistles carried on the breeze, mingling with the chatter of local birds. Rising intervals of sound that held an ominous intensity.

Life was filled with circumstances beyond your control—this was not a news flash. Every winning streak, however magical, held a crash at its end. A fate not directed solely at his heart like a poisoned arrow, but one universally doled out by the roll of DNA and its ever-failing replication over time: your telomeres frayed, everything blurred and faded. Slowly, he'd come around to "let go and let God" and all the other catchphrases of a twelve-step world. But the glancing of Rachel's arm against his as they ambled along gave Paul the giddy feeling of a last-minute save of his own divining. He felt outside of time, both cautious and reckless, felt the pure hit of the charge between them. A shimmering sense of his best possible self and the challenge of tangling with a formidable player. As though all this time he hadn't been building a new life with Celeste, but merely waiting for his old one to reassemble itself into its intended design, for himself to reappear within it.

They came to a bend where the giraffes were still a ways back from the fence but in clear view. They settled on a bench, and a trio of giraffes began to drift closer in a twining pyramid of long necks and legs.

"Mesmerizing, aren't they?" Rachel said.

"They look so polite. With their little hooves."

"So languid and velvety."

She leaned forward from the waist, rolling her neck and shoulders in the same fluid motion as the giraffes, and slowly rose from the bench. Paul told himself he was imagining this, but the animals' focus seemed to shift toward her in curiosity. Rachel looked back at him and grinned, then began walking toward the fence, her arms alternately bending and extending in a kind of hula dance. She held her head high, drawing it forward and back in articulate isolations, her wrists delicately flexing in imitation of the giraffes' ankles, her gait matching theirs somehow, despite the difference in scale and number of feet on the ground.

As though choreographed, two of the giraffes peeled off to the side, and the third stepped forward all the way to the fence, close enough for Paul to see the nicks and scrapes on its haunches, the welt of an insect bite on its skin, the fraying tail. He could smell its animal funk, a pungent barn-like odor of shit and straw, could sense the tough, dry bristles of cropped mane as if he were running his palm down its length. At the center of each irregular brown shape was a small marking, a thread star of lighter hair. For a moment, this immediate pattern of brown blotches against a cream background filled his vision like a mortared wall of stones; then he felt a pulse of fear—a peripheral movement snapping him to attention. With a great swoop, the giraffe bent its neck over the top of the fence, its head barely a foot above Rachel's. One liquid brown eye gazed at her with uncanny intensity. Paul could see the thick lashes, could feel the giraffe's attempt to categorize her: not zookeeper, but not the other either. Some kind of recognition seemed to pass between them, between Rachel and the giraffe, but he was outside of it, able only to see it happening, not experience the exchange.

The giraffe drew its head up, the long neck arched, its lips pointed to the sky, then drew it forward and nipped at its flank. Straightening once more to full height, it looked beyond them toward the rest of the zoo, its gaze settled back into captive placidity. Locating the other giraffes, it moved slowly toward them with what looked to Paul like defeat.

Rachel turned back to him now, her expression wistful as she crossed her arms. A light had gone out of her too, but he understood why she'd wanted to come. The particularity of the giraffes and how the broad expanse of pattern in motion was both miraculous and soothing. Beyond physical attraction, a shared visual sensibility—this pleasure in color and shape, in motion and line—had been the greater part of what drew him, what brought him back to Rachel over and over again. Where did he stand in the world if he wasn't giving form to those ideas? When she sat down beside him again, he said, "I haven't been making anything for a while."

She slouched and let her head rest on the bench. "Breakups are hard. Looks like I owe you five bucks."

In a roving tangle of their own, three of the kids from the gate pushed and prodded each other along. "Just ask them," said the girl, in the kind of giggling, stoned whisper that's no whisper at all.

"You ask them," said the boy in question, ducking away from her elbow as she tried to nudge him toward the bench. The movement threw him off-balance, and he stumbled, going down hard on one knee.

Rachel leaned forward, asking if the boy was all right, and Paul held his hand on her thigh to keep her from rising.

"What are you doing?" she said, and he let go.

"Markson, you're a spaz," said the other boy.

Markson looked up at the girl, then at Rachel. "The penguins," he said. "We're trying to find the penguins."

Rachel said, "Go back to the monkeys and hang a right."

Paul looked at her, startled by her certainty.

"Cameron," she said. "He liked the penguins too."

"I told you this was wrong," said the other boy, slowly walking backward in the direction they'd come. His thumb and index finger at his mouth, he feigned inhaling a joint. "Day's a wasting."

The girl pulled Markson to his feet. "You're such a lug."

Markson flashed Paul an impish grin and tore off, the other boy falling in step as the girl ran cursing behind them.

"Not as good as the giraffes," Paul said. "But almost."

"Did you love her?" Rachel asked.

"Who—Celeste?"

"Hm. Pretty name."

Paul suddenly heard the way he must've sounded—as though he'd been surprised by the idea rather than the question, which held him now. Celeste's absence left him feeling aimless and bleak. But did he love her?

"Not really," he said. "Not the way she wanted. Why would you ask that?"

Rachel was silent. Then she said, "I like to hear that it can happen. Even if it doesn't work out."

Paul imagined the kid, Markson, twenty years from now, working some meaningless job, remembering a girl whose touch he'd skittered away from one sunny afternoon at the zoo, with no recollection of the hulking man beside a sad, pale woman who'd known where to find the penguins, or of the other friends he'd left behind at the gate.

"Two-fifty," said Paul.

"What's that?"

"Your bet. Only half the kids came in."

Rachel settled back on the bench, letting her head rest against him this time. She said, "Do you ever just feel so tired?"

Folding his arm around her, he smoothed the curls back from her forehead. The giraffes had moved beyond their line of sight, leaving a clear shot of lawn and a few oddly placed boulders. At his back, he could feel the cooler ocean air that within the hour would be drawn to the sun-warmed land, whitening the sky; the tops of Monterey pines and eucalyptus, the crowns of tattered palms now so sharply drawn would fade from focus, their outlines blurred by descending fog.

"Only when I'm awake," said Paul.

More than hearing it, he felt the exhalation of her laughter in the twitch of her body against his side, a sensation he couldn't help but savor. When he first knew Rachel, his use of coke was an occasional thing, left over from his art school days. If someone showed up at an opening or a significant birthday with a small fold of origami paper, he wasn't one to say no. But he'd have shelled out cash, in those early days, only to celebrate a major accomplishment. His first commissions. His first group show. He wasn't predisposed to addiction, had no tragic family history. He'd just eased himself into it one packet at a time, with a fateful discovery. He liked working high, much preferring coke's edge to the lush numbness of pot—though he could see the draw of being stoned at the zoo.

Weed was a teenage rite of passage, a fine enough balm for life's killing tedium. But the luxury of coke marked his artistic arrival, Rachel one of several women he'd become involved with on that cusp, all introduced to him by friends. Before her, a high school history teacher; directly after, a stringer for the *San Jose Mercury News*. Each duly impressed by his talent and fledgling fame. Only Rachel's admiration had been tempered by a competitive nature and a demand for equal recognition of her own success.

There were opportunities that came your way, any number of

potential fortunes eager to be tagged with your name. All he'd had to do was see. To keep shepherding a cascade of ideas from pencil sketch into full dimension. His very being reflected and transformed—a crystallization for those primed to pay handsomely for it. No one was going to beg you. But if you brought it forth, tore it into existence; if you sawed and hammered, etched and painted, what was yours alone, building on all that came before you; if you brought those objects to light, beaming and shining into the world, it would crack joyfully open on your behalf. Or so he'd believed.

He'd been greedy—yes. But the art world expected it, demanded that of you. His raw desire the force that helped him endure the boredom of the Sausalito Art Festival, where the well-known comic had idly struck up conversation. Not at the table displaying Paul's small-scale pieces—the wooden toys, the decorative frames and platters that once offset his bills—but at the stand selling fresh lemonade. The comic—Russ, as he would come to know him—sweating profusely in the September sun, and relieved, Paul imagined, that rather than gawk, he'd simply nodded in acknowledgment of the heat and the endless line. Two grown men, determined to slake their thirst on the tang of childhood memory rather than any offering of local vineyards or breweries.

"Maker or buyer?" Russ asked, and Paul had soon felt him sheltering in their conversation, had helplessly grinned at the bits he spun, fiercely characterizing both artists and patrons, the sulky festival workers in blue T-shirts giving directions to the Porta Potties, all topped off with his son's tantrum at the Ben and Jerry's booth when they'd run out of Cherry Garcia. A secretive flood of half-volume asides driven into Paul's ears until he could hardly breathe for laughing. And when Russ showed up at his table later, pocketed a promo card for his upcoming show at a Los Angeles gallery, Paul had a magnificent feeling. This would be the start of his destined ascent, of the success he'd always held as his due.

"Your true oeuvre, I presume," Russ said, tweezing out the words in the voice of a pretentious critic, and then dropping it to say, "Seriously, man—it's a pleasure to meet you." He gestured at the tents and tables. "This sort of thing's my wife's idea of fine art, but I occasionally invest—as my accountant would say—though I prefer collect. We live up here now, in this bastion of wealth and hippie residue, though most of my work's still in L.A. My dealer too. Did I say dealer? I meant the clubs. Clubs, hearts, aces, lucky star."

Russ, it would turn out, had done his own time in rehab, his commission a fairy-tale wish whose dark consequences only granting would reveal. Not just a single or a pair of pieces, but an entire bedroom: one enormous connected installation that was furniture and playground rolled into one. A loft bed and a slide whose side wall masked a secret hideout. Wardrobe and dresser, built-in bookshelves and desk, every surface decorated in Paul's style but themed to suit the boy. He remembered showing Rachel some of the early sketches that she'd said reminded her of an amusement park. He'd put all of who he was into that work—the piece was him—and he'd destroyed it. Not Russ, not anyone else.

Paul stood up and, at Rachel's suggestion, they walked the rest of the loop around what was billed as the African savanna, an illusion spoiled in his mind—more than anything else—by the verdant mown grass. Beside a bare stretch of fence, a woman with a scarf tied around her head and what looked to be a hand-knitted sweater had set up an easel and a collapsible stool. A cluster of visitors had gathered to watch. She'd already laid in the large central mound of cast-cement boulders in soft brown washes and was working on the details of a grazing zebra, the foreground still blank as though she, too, were holding out for some other color than that virulent green.

As they moved past, Paul said, "I feel bad for the zebra. That woman's stealing whatever thunder he's got left. She's looking at him, sure, but everyone else is watching her paint—and I use that word loosely."

"That woman," said Rachel, "is sick. You didn't see the head scarf? How thin she was? At least she's working."

Paul glanced back. "Maybe she's just a skinny woman with bad taste in clothes."

"I should be at the hospital with Lily."

"It's not because of Celeste. I'd already stopped before I met her—working, among other things."

Rachel veered toward the low outer fence, crossed her forearms on its broad sloping rail, a thick plastic slab meant to look like wood. Inside the fence, a peacock sauntered past, its tail feathers folded and dragging through the grass. Without looking at him, she said, "Maybe now is the time to back up."

He leaned on the rail beside her, not knowing where to begin. "Wasn't there some tiger that escaped and killed a guy? Siberian tiger, I think it was. Jumped the moat and the wall. At least they've got walls for the tigers, right?"

Still staring out into the pen, Rachel sighed and shook her head.

"Right," said Paul. "I did a stint in rehab and haven't made anything since." This got her attention, as he'd known it would, but when she turned and said only, "Oh, Paul," the sorrow in her voice unnerved him. What was it he'd expected? That she'd be impressed?

Slowly, he spun out the major details. The triumph of his second group show in L.A., followed by a succession of disappointments. The interested dealer who ultimately didn't take him on. The solo show that never materialized, despite reviews touting his originality and promise. And finally, fatefully, the cancelation of Russ's commission after a year's worth of work. Not by Russ's choice, or even the kid's—sometimes Paul felt he could've lived with that. But on the final, killing whim of Annalise, Russ's still new and much younger wife, a brash and already bitter woman whose good qualities, assuming she had any, escaped him.

She hadn't liked Paul, that much was clear, and though she'd expressed a begrudging admiration for his work, she questioned every choice he made, argued about scale and proportion, about storage space. To her it was kitchen cabinets, and she'd likely have preferred to furnish the bedroom with matching pieces from Pottery Barn, which, for all he knew, was what she'd done. It wasn't even her kid. Paul still thought of him that way, as the boy, though of course he knew his name was Kevin. That Russ would cave, that he'd strung him along, that he hadn't held his ground on Paul's behalf, on behalf of the work—which he'd known was good. That had cut him deeply. And the compromises he'd made to please Annalise. Drawings she'd wrinkled her nose at, entire sections he'd been made to rebuild. Even now, he couldn't think about it without breaking into a sweat, without the urge to put his fist through glass, through a wall, without a desire to track her down and flatten her.

All of this, he told Rachel, coinciding with the reappearance of an old high school friend, who'd shown up on Paul's doorstep with his dealer in tow, looking for a place to crash for a weekend that turned into a month. Glowing nights of pharmaceutical coke and cognac quickly giving way to lesser grades that still emptied his bank account, unearthing a predisposition for mania. The street dealers and assorted partying strangers that had replaced his friends, camping out in and trashing his house. How he'd taken a Sawzall to the completed sections of the bedroom piece—the culminating act of three days without sleep that landed him, raving and covered in sawdust, in the emergency room. The colleague of his father's who'd vouched for his care, prescribing the lithium that had brought him down and managing to place him in the thirty-day program at Alta Mira rather than the locked ward of a hospital. Sobriety and the solidity of custom cabinetwork, of his life with Celeste, cutting out the highs and lows for the safety of the middle.

"I suppose," Paul said, finally, "we all have to grow up."

"So you've been busy, then—since I saw you last."

Paul laughed in surprise, finding her quip equally sharp and sympathetic. "That's not really funny."

"No," said Rachel. "Hardly anything is."

Without thinking, he leaned in and kissed her, his hands slipping under the hem of her shirt to take hold of her waist. She kissed him back, but as they settled and then pulled apart, she said, "That's one way to get me to shut up."

What he'd wanted was to pull her inside him, to mix her pain, past and present, with his own—not to silence her. High in every respect, it had been easy to destroy the kid's bedroom, the first cut into the painted wood like a release from his body, his life. But the crash—the crash had nearly killed him, and there'd been no easy walking away from the coke or his work. There were slips and residual manic escalations; he'd had to relinquish a part of himself to go on. It was Celeste who was good about triggers and keeping clean boundaries drawn—it wasn't until he met her that he'd understood how it could be done, that you made a choice. He hadn't chosen Celeste—not the way she needed, not the way she wished. Wasn't that the reason she was moving on? He didn't know if he could choose Rachel, either, if there was still a chance between them—but he couldn't go back to his work. He wasn't ready, might not ever be.

Paul said, "I wasn't trying—"

"I know. You just caught me off guard. What are you doing, then—with all your time?"

"I just kissed you."

"I was there."

"I was there? That's all you've got?"

"Paul—don't put too much on it. This day—you can see . . ." She dragged her hand down her face and sighed. "I don't know what you want."

This quieted him. He looked out across the fenced paddock and felt the rise and fall of his own breath. "I want to see those Siberian tigers."

They followed the signs to the big cat enclosures, small oases of plants thinning out to bare cement that angled steeply down into a waterless moat, but the animals were nowhere to be seen. Circling around, they came to a squat flat-topped building, its cream stucco heavily bloomed with gray stains. Below the mosaicked red letters spelling LION HOUSE were three matching sets of red doors, each bearing a heavy round silver ring.

"A little mausoleum-like," Rachel said. "Don't you think?"

Paul nodded, but he was thinking of those vacant doorways outside the parking lot. She stepped to the middle door, had to leverage the weight of her body to pull it open. Inside the hushed cavernous space, the air was close and reeking. The open central area verged on darkness, but the perimeter of the cell-like cages was infused with the theatrical yellow of sun pouring down through unexpected skylights. A young woman was pushing a stroller, her voice resounding as she explained to her fussing son that the big kitties were having their nap.

All the animals did seem to be sleeping, their backs turned toward the bars. Only a jaguar, in a cruelly small cage, paced back and forth.

He thought of Rousseau's jungle paintings, the lions and tigers wide-eyed. Images so popular they'd become clichéd, but he still held a particular fondness for those works, whose decorative elements had hooked his interest as a kid. Down the route of creation was ruin now; he'd find himself wretched and caged, sleeping his days away waiting for someone to bring him a pail of meat. Walking a few feet ahead, Rachel paused in front of the cheetah, its spotted body draped across a cement branch whose flat brown color had clearly been brushed straight from the can. Couldn't they do any better than that? Paul came up behind her, wanted to slip his arms around her waist, but it seemed crude to touch her amid the stench and the murmuring echoes reflected off the terracotta tiles. He replayed the kiss in his head, gaining no further clarity on where they stood.

"It's a little depressing in here," she said. "Whose idea was it to come to the zoo?"

Distracted by the squeal of hinges, the shuffle of entering footsteps halted by a sharp sneaker squeak, he failed to deliver a comeback.

"Aw, shit," someone said, and Paul turned to see the posse of kids.

"Stinks in here," the girl said, and Markson shushed her.

"Don't shush me," she said, giving him a little shove.

With only the one way in or out, the young woman steered her stroller toward the door farthest from the one where the kids still hovered, her child wailing in protest.

Rachel snorted. "Inevitable, I suppose."

"They look dead," said Markson's friend, scanning the cages. "Except for him. What is that, a cougar?"

"Jaguar, stupid," said the girl.

"Penguins?" asked Paul.

"No," said Rachel. "I think I'm ready to go."

Like poles along the same axis, the kids shifted away from them as they moved toward the exit. "Maybe," she said, "one last look at the giraffes."

"Whatever you want," Paul said, reaching his hand above her head to push open the door.

By the time they'd looped back to the giraffes, the fog had blown in, erasing the enchanting contrast of bright sun and deep shadow. The light was bleak and diffused now, the day quickly fading.

"I never get used to that," said Rachel. "The way the weather just turns." She tapped her index finger on a plaque with worn photos of the animals. "African storks, it says. We didn't see any storks. Bernal Heights is probably more like Africa than this right now. This is the worst possible climate for everything here."

"Except maybe the squirrels."

"We didn't see any squirrels either."

Paul stood beside her at the rail. The giraffes had migrated to a weathered wooden building where they hung about like cows waiting to be let into the barn.

"Another day's work over," he said.

"When I was in fifth grade," Rachel said, "I read this book. Scholastic Services—remember those skimpy little paperbacks? Except I could never find it again, kept looking for it in my mother's basement—everything else was there. *Call of the Wild* moldering alongside *Mr. Popper's Penguins*. Must've been something I took out from the library. About these two girls with nothing in common—from different neighborhoods, different groups at school. But they run into each other, right? On the outskirts of town."

“The outskirts of town?”

“Past wherever they were allowed to go. There’s this scraggly bit of land, an unused tract, and they keep ending up there at the same time. And they have these sort of experiences—no, not like that. Just let me finish, okay? Things to do with scale. A colony of ants would be running over a patch of weeds, and as they watched, they’d have the shared feeling of moving down into that rushing ant world. Or they’d become, for just a minute or two, the movement of the water in some sewer runoff, the floating leaves, the bits of twig. They’d be transmuted into these other beings, these other forms. One day they find this rock with a flat piece of metal sticking out, like the broken tip of a sword, and if they hold the metal together, they can pull the piece free, and it’s like a spell. They’re still standing in the same place—”

“The not-African-savanna.”

“Yes—only it’s centuries ago, in King Arthur’s time.”

“They go back in time?”

“No, no, no—it’s more . . . it’s like a shared vision. But they don’t ever talk about it. They just know that they’ve been in this other place that’s simultaneous, or overlapping somehow. And it happens a couple of times. Then they start missing each other. One comes down and the other doesn’t show—neither of them knows where the other one lives—and the thing, whatever it was that they held between them, is gone.”

“And that’s the end?”

“Yeah. Their season’s over, I guess. Or they’re quickly too old for that kind of play—like an end of childhood thing. Or there was just enough magic for them each to go on with their separate lives. Or who the fuck knows—I’ve never been able to find it again.”

Paul tilted his boot up against the fence, pressed his weight into the ball of his foot. “You don’t think we have anything in common?”

"No, we do—we do. But it's like all we've got is some little scrap of metal. Nothing that stands up in the real world."

"Are you talking about me or Lily?"

"We should go. I think we're the only people left in the zoo."

"There's probably some kind of siren, but we can go if you want."

"A siren."

"An announcement, a bell, zookeepers in little green jeeps. Everybody out of the zoo."

"I don't think that's what zookeepers do."

"Not everybody dies," he said.

"No?"

"All right, everybody dies. But some people make it through treatment. Some people do well."

"That what they tell you in NA?"

"I remembered you as nicer," he said.

She shrugged. "People change."

On the drive back, they were mostly silent; Paul hadn't expected her to ask him in. Rachel flipped on the light as they came up the stairs, and he thought once more of the lady and the tiger, though the doors were all open now. The leaves of the corn plant brought to mind Rousseau's painting again. Its pair of lions, their yellow-ringed eyes round with fear or curiosity, charmed by the music of the dark figure standing in between, either leading them forward or drawing them back. The nude woman on a velvet chaise that he'd found so startling as a boy, her placid nakedness more unnerving than arousing, otherworldly somehow, which of course it was—*Il Sogno*, the dream, he'd later learned it was called. The centrally placed lion, the musician in striped skirt, and the half-hidden profile of a foraging elephant all stare out of the picture plane, their gaze, he'd thought, directed at him as if to say, *We see you and we see you looking too.*

When he was a kid, that flattened jungle with its waxen-looking flowers and leaves, its hidden monkeys and deep velvety shadows, the small bright moon in a barely blue sky, had reminded him of museum dioramas and their illusory backgrounds. He'd never cared to interpret the painting's meaning. There were critics and art historians aplenty to busy themselves with Rousseau's intent. Paul preferred to indulge, striving to maintain his own visceral sense of the work as both peaceful and unsettling, a world that both beckoned and warned him away. And yet, as with the facets of any dream, his mind drew things together: the rank lion house at the zoo, the avocado-green tones of the carpeting at his feet and the decade they invoked, the jungle-like leaves of the corn plant that had summoned back the painting.

"It's a peculiar layout," Paul said. He began to comment on the wasted space of the hallway, but Rachel cut him off.

"What was that?"

He peered into the darkened passage leading to the kitchen where her attention was turned, heard the ambient hum of the house, his own breath in the silence. "If anything, it's strangely quiet."

"No—I distinctly heard something, like the clink of a glass."

"Monsters under the bed," said Paul, heading into the passageway just the same. "I'll go see."

"Wait," she said. "*Paul.*" But he'd already moved into the kitchen, where the stove seemed whitely luminescent.

The back door was open, a darker rectangle of night, crossed by the faint, painted railing of the small wooden deck Rachel crowded with planters. Not seeing any knives, he grabbed the tea kettle from the stove and strode across the linoleum, assuring himself that whoever had been through was long gone. He recoiled in horror, his voice caught in his throat, as a figure reached out, kept him from tumbling down the steep wooden steps into the darkness of the yard.

"Whoa, take it easy! I'm unarmed."

The voice was wry, its tone familiar, and the figure slowly resolved into Frank.

"I do seem to have a way of taking you by surprise—you all right?" Frank reached down toward the deck, and Paul heard the small clink of a ring against a bottle. "Anchor Steam," he said. "Couple more in the fridge. What'd you do with Rachel?"

"I'm right here. Jesus, Frank—you couldn't turn on a light? I was just about to dial 911."

"Yeah, your friend Paul here tried to take me out with the kettle. Nearly took a header down the stairs—saved your life there, buddy, didn't I?"

"Nice weapon," Rachel said. "Give me that. You all right?"

Paul's heart was still beating fast, and before he could answer, she'd turned to Frank.

"You told me you were having dinner with Miguel. How was Lily—how'd it go?"

"It went. I am. He's meeting me here."

"I thought he would meet you at the hospital. We could've picked you up."

"It's fine. I'm fine. Lily is fine. We're all fine."

"So it was terrible."

"Yeah. Pretty bad."

Paul thought of Lily descending the stairs, his erroneous assumption of her pregnancy a mistake sharpened by Frank's despair. She'd been pregnant here before, bearing them the boy whose glow-in-the-dark stars still graced the ceiling of Rachel's studio. Of course they'd come to her house, where their life was once happy and filled with hope. Lily in that moment on the landing, as he remembered it now, bore a resemblance to Celeste in femininity and style—a woman whose course in life was unaffected by his presence. *You're not the taxi.* Her stubborn grip on the rail, her polarizing force holding Rachel and Frank in place at the door.

Now here Paul was, trying to deepen his breath, feeling ungainly and oversized as he squeezed himself down onto a splintery tread, his back pressed into the stanchions. A few steps above him, Rachel half reclined against the house, her extended legs crossed, her profile turned toward her friend. After dragging it free from the pots of sword plants and spilling nasturtiums, Frank had resettled in the canvas director's chair at the lip of the stairs, a sculpted form against the sky, like the piper emerging from Rousseau's jungle.

"I wouldn't rest your whole weight against those posts," Frank said.

"That's rude," said Rachel.

"Not if you want him to live. This whole deck is rotting—I nearly split off the top rail when I came out earlier, and I wasn't leaning that hard. In the daylight you can see how the whole staircase is pulling away from the house."

Paul shifted one foot to the step below him and straightened his back. Pushing his hand against one of the stanchions, he could feel the soft splintering give of the wood from the nails, the peeling layers of paint damp beneath his palm.

"And yet," she said, "we're all sitting out here."

"It's a beautiful night. What do you say, Paul, my man?"

"You could take out that railing with a couple of good kicks. You should talk to your landlord, Rachel."

"I'm sure he'll run right over here and build me a new one."

"Maybe you should ask Paul to do it—isn't he handy that way? I could use a project. We could do it together."

"Funny," she said, "I'm not really concerned about the deck right now."

"No," said Frank. "Nobody is."

"Let me have some of that," Rachel said, and Frank passed her his beer. "You think Lily is ever going to stop being mad at me?"

"I think she left your to-go cup in the cab," Frank said. "Since they were five, Paul—that's how long they've been friends. But they refuse to exchange Christmas presents."

"I thought you were Jewish," Paul said.

"She is. They are. Chanukah, whatever—that's not the point. They don't exchange birthday presents either. But you can see that we're here. Because that's what friendship is. She's mad at you, Ray, because she knows you can take it."

"I don't know if I can."

"Well, you've got your friend Paul here; he seems like a good guy. What'd you two get up to all afternoon?"

"Stop saying his name over and over, will you?" Rachel passed Frank the bottle. "We went to the zoo."

Frank snickered and then finished the beer. "So a really good guy."

"I don't know about 'really.' He's on the rebound. I was supposed to be his comfort. His sympathy lay. What was her name again? Cecily?"

"Celeste."

"How long were you married?" asked Frank.

"Not married," Paul said. "Just together. For about a year."

"But he didn't love her. Or doesn't think he did."

"That's a fine line," Frank said. "What was it?"

Paul tried to think how he'd wound up here in the dark, Rachel and Frank on the steps above him. He would've liked a beer. The bottle cool in his hand, the bitter taste breaking on his tongue, carbonation scraping the back of his throat. "I don't know."

"But you like him," Frank said, "even still."

"It would seem that I do. I always liked his work. But then I tend to be drawn to narcissistic men."

The director's chair creaked as Frank leaned forward. "Didn't you used to have a list? No lawyers, no musicians . . ."

"No bass players, I believe it was."

"Celeste was a cellist—is a cellist," Paul said.

"They met in NA—or am I not supposed to say that?"

"A good story for the grandkids," Frank said.

"Except they didn't get married."

"So he said. What time is it? I'm beginning to think Miguel's not coming."

"I had feelings for Celeste," Paul said, aware of the loudness of his voice, of the way it bounced off the siding of the house next door.

"I never said you didn't," Rachel said.

"It just wasn't . . . we weren't . . ."

"Not everything works out," Frank said. "You don't have to explain."

"I couldn't believe my luck, you know? She made it seem easy. Easier." To stay clean, he wanted to say, but instead he said, "To start over."

"Paul sank his boat with too much coke. And now he doesn't think he can make things."

"Not without a slip. Not what I made before."

Frank said, "And that's why cello dumped him."

"*No,*" Paul said. "No. She wanted us . . . I thought she wanted more. That's what I've been telling myself. But maybe she didn't want anything at all."

"Like a koan," Frank said. "What's the sound of one hand not wanting? Seems an enviable state."

"*Frank*," said Rachel, softly.

His forearm lay across the wooden arm of the chair, and the empty beer bottle hung loose in his hand, his ring finger clinking out the rhythm of a song. "Anchor Steam beer," he said, as though trying on lyrics. "I thought you didn't like hoppy brews."

"I don't. I got those for you."

"She's a lovely hostess, Paul, isn't she?"

The doorbell rang through the house, a persistent and buzzing alarm that made Paul think of bank vaults and prison doors clanging shut on television dramas—he half expected sirens to follow.

"That'd be his royal highness," Frank said. He set down the empty bottle and rolled the band of his watch around his wrist. Pinching the face between his thumb and forefinger, he brought it closer to his own, and a faint blue light fell across his chin. "Only forty-five minutes late."

Rachel rose.

"Stay," Frank said, pushing himself up and past her, through the kitchen doorway, in a single motion. "I'll let him in."

Rachel took his place in the director's chair.

"Miguel is . . . ?" Paul said.

"Frank's crony from high school."

"So like you and Lily then."

"More like partners in crime. Breaking into abandoned buildings and dropping shit from the freeway overpass. Scoring weed, scoring girls. Whatever it was you could do, growing up in Stockton, to be badass without getting arrested, though Frank did a little time for possession. *Back in the day*—or whatever you want to call it. Lily was never a big fan. They don't usually see each other but every few years."

Light spilled into the kitchen from the living room, and a moment later Frank appeared in the doorway alone, a denim jacket in his hand. He smiled, swaying slightly.

"He's double-parked—we're just going to go. Don't wait up, Ray—you know Miguel, we'll probably wind up—" The insistent honking of a car horn interrupted. "Jesus, he's such a pain." Frank kissed Rachel on the forehead; then, reaching his hand down to Paul, he said, "It was good to meet you."

"Likewise," Paul said, the word overridden by another long honk. He'd had to lean forward to catch Frank's hand, which was warm, the palm smooth and dry against his own, and in those few seconds of contact, he felt a surge of emotion, a disorienting blend of affection and grief.

"I like him," Paul said, once they were alone.

"Most people do." Rachel got up and set the chair back in its place at the far end of the deck. "I suppose you'll be going back now, over your infamous bridge?" Light from the doorway cast half her body in shadow. Paul came up the stairs to meet her, and she stepped into his arms.

"I could stay if you want me to."

"No," she said. "It'd just be harder tomorrow."

He kissed her and felt the give of her body against his. Then she pulled away.

"Well," she said. "Thanks for stopping by."

He laughed, and then she said, "No—really."

"Well," Paul said, unable to keep the bite from his voice. "Then I guess I'm going now."

She placed her hand lightly on his chest. "I'll walk you to the door."

"That's gracious of you."

"Like Frank said—I'm a lovely hostess."

"Rachel."

"What?"

Paul couldn't think of what it was that he wanted to say. He'd had no right, he could see that now—what did he expect, coming here on a whim? "Let me know how it goes with Lily."

"I can do that."

He gestured toward the kitchen. "After you."

In the foyer, they paused as Paul checked for his keys. Then he followed her one more time down the steps to the door. "So," he said. "This was fun."

"Was it?"

"Parts of it were, don't you think? The giraffes. Those ridiculous kids."

"The giraffes were good."

He bent to kiss her goodbye, but she stiffened. He shut his eyes and shook his head.

"Paul," she said softly. "Don't . . ."

He waited, cramped together with her in the stairwell, but she didn't go on.

"Don't feel bad? Don't get mad? Don't ever darken your door? What, Rachel, what?"

"Don't leave, all right? Don't go."

She sank down onto the carpeted step and put a hand over her eyes.

"All right," he said. "All right—I gotcha." He slid his arm under her knees and carried her back upstairs.

* *

Whatever he'd imagined driving across the bridge that morning, the intensity between them in bed had outdone his recollection. But now, with the light from a sodium streetlamp splashing peculiar patterns across the sheets, Paul heard the sound of a car door slam and felt uneasy. He'd dozed off but didn't think she had.

Rachel lay on her side, her body turned away from him. With the tips of his fingers, he traced the curve of her shoulder, the ridged span of her rib cage, her skin softer, smoother still in the deep indentation of her waist, where he felt a shivery tension in the muscle below. He didn't have it in him to go again, so he let his hand come to rest on the shelf of her hip.

"Frank," she said, and Paul thought she was calling him by the other man's name. Then he, too, heard the key in the lock, the metallic ruffling of the blinds as they swung, first with the opening, and then again with the gentle closing of the front door, a man coming up the familiar staircase of what had once been his home.

"Is it that late?" asked Paul.

Rachel reached for the clock on her nightstand, a flea market find, if he remembered correctly, with a forties-style floral embellishment painted on the drawer. Then she said something he didn't quite hear.

"What was that?"

"The witching hour," she said. "Nearly midnight."

He let his gaze drift around the dim room. The walls of her studio were one thing, but in the rest of her apartment, she'd hung framed artwork, the originals of her own licensed work mixed in with that of her friends. In her bedroom the walls were bare.

"Kind of stark in here," he said, mindful of the volume of his voice. Though from the ringing silence that had followed the labored steps of his entrance, he imagined Frank, who hadn't so much as used the bathroom or turned on a light, was passed out on the couch with his clothes and maybe even his cowboy boots on.

"You're giving tips on interior decoration now?"

He patted her hip. "Just an observation."

"Paul," she said.

"Yeah?"

"Did you just pat my hip?"

"No, I don't know—why?"

"Nothing," Rachel said.

But he knew what she meant: a gesture without romantic feeling.

"The rest of the place is so busy," she went on, "and I like that, you know? All the rhythms and juxtapositions of line and shape, like calligraphy. But I wanted one blank canvas for the light to move across, one room where I didn't have to think. A space of respite."

"Very poetic," Paul said, and she sighed. He spooned against her, one arm beneath, the other wrapped around her waist. "Sorry. A reflex, I suppose."

"To dispel the feeling."

"To say something clever. You do the same."

"Let's not . . ."

"No, I wasn't—I didn't mean to."

"I'm exhausted," she said. "Are you staying?"

"I thought I would," said Paul, though he hadn't until she'd asked. "If you want me to."

"It's up to you."

He brought the top sheet up over their legs. "We had a good day, didn't we?"

"We did." She pulled his arm more snugly around her and nestled in. "Wake me up if you go."

"I won't."

"But if you do."

"All right."

She patted his hand, and Paul let out a small breath of laughter.

With each deepening inhale, the warmth of her expanded. Paul thought of Celeste, tall and lithe, all bony hips and angles to Rachel's soft curves, how each of them dressed against their natural attributes. Where the vanity in Celeste's bedroom was strewn with cosmetics, with bangles and earrings, bottles of perfume, Rachel's dresser was made of unfinished pine, a ghostly rectangle against the blank wall, topped with stacks of books. Rachel could use a good set of shelves; he knew he'd never build them. Her grip on his arm gave way, and Paul rolled onto his back. What had he come here for? Had he hoped to retrieve something of greater value? Or simply blot another thing out? Anything to fill his desire, his need—no matter the destruction. Anything to feel good, if only for the moment.

"Did you keep the drawings?" Rachel said, her voice low and blurred.

"I thought you were asleep."

"Almost," she said, then a few seconds later, "Did you?"

"From the kid's bedroom? No."

She turned and settled her head on his shoulder, rested her hand on his chest. "I'm sorry," she said.

"I know." Paul shifted his arm beneath her back, pressed her to his side. "It's all right."

"You'll try again. You will. Us too."

Rachel's body grew heavy as she drifted off. He'd torn up the drawings the minute Russ and Annalise had left his studio that day. Earlier versions still inhabited his sketchbooks—he hadn't thought to go that far. Ecstatic doodles and tracing-paper cutouts stuck between the pages of countless black bound journals, sketches for the pieces he'd sold buried in the scrap pile of unfinished ideas.

He'd seen a photo of the boy, of Russ's kid, Kevin, straw haired with expectant blue eyes. Had tried to build him an interior landscape: a joyful, decorated place to match his simple dreams of trucks and sailboats and the family dog—an old Dalmatian named Jake. A place to sleep. To do homework. To play. And beneath the brightly colored slide, a secret place to hide his dark longings from the world.

CHANCES ARE | 1992

In the Au Bon Pain at Fifty-Third Street, a baker rolls out a cart of warm pastries, and the scent of yeast and almonds fills the air. What Richard would really like is a cigarette, though he quit smoking ages ago. Downing half a cappuccino has only fueled his uneasy anticipation of seeing Rachel.

It'd be rude to have his pastry now, before she arrives, but as the baker slides a tray into the display, Richard can almost taste the first flaky bite. He starts to get up, then sees Rachel through the glass, her smile widening in mistaken assumption that he's risen on her behalf. Has he ever gotten things right where she was concerned? It's what he means to do today—no matter that years have passed and they've managed to maintain a friendship anyway.

Maybe the passage of time itself is what impels him to tell her how sorry he's always been for the way their one evening together played out. He's married to Lena now, and they have a kid, and Rachel seems content in her own life, out in California. Nevertheless, it's stuck with him that what must've seemed callous and self-serving was never intended that way. He'd come quickly, then reached for his cigarettes, shamed on both counts when she said a lingering smell of smoke would arouse suspicion. Aroused. That was what he had been. Not to mention guilt-ridden—Lena waiting at home in his tiny apartment, only a few blocks away. So nervous before, then ashamed of his performance after, he'd done nothing, given Rachel nothing in return. A realization whose weight only hit him later, once he was home, Lena tucked beside him in their Murphy bed.

The furnished apartment where his years-delayed yet seemingly fated assignation with Rachel had taken place was just off the Hudson, its briny summer scent rising with the memory, souring the stronger aromas of coffee and baked goods. A few days before she and her longtime boyfriend were due to move into subsidized housing in Richard's neighborhood, he'd run into her near Sheridan Square. After a beer at the White Horse, they'd been reluctant to part, and a few days later, speaking by phone for the very first time, they arranged to meet at her still-vacant two-bedroom apartment with its noted back patio and river view, so conveniently close to the overpriced and nearly windowless mousehole of a studio he shared with Lena.

On the designated evening, he'd met Rachel with trepidation in front of The Duchess, taxis tearing past them through the dusk, as though testing their choice to cross the avenue. But when they ventured into the sheltered dark of Grove Street, a cheerfulness buoyed them toward the river. Nearing her building, a vague and impossible fantasy briefly floated between them, as if they might elude their current partners but keep the spoils of Manhattan real estate. And though that spacious apartment would remain available to them for several more days after their awkward consummation, he and Rachel didn't speak, let alone return.

Then two, maybe three years later, they'd found themselves once again living in apartment buildings mere blocks apart, the vagaries of affordable rents landing them close to the East River, in the fifties this time. A coincidence that made for chance meetings in which they'd happily walk a common stretch, catching up on the present without reference to that troubling encounter. Rachel was living alone, and they easily returned to their original ongoing conversation about art, speaking avidly on the corner of Second Avenue about capturing light and the influence of artists whose work continued to inspire them. It wasn't until she'd moved out to San Francisco, when only a semiannual gig or seeing family drew her back East, that they'd begun to meet for coffee at Au Bon Pain, where Rachel was partial to the apricot pastry.

Walking up from the subway at Fifty-Third Street, Rachel wondered at her compulsion, after so many years, to meet up with Richard whenever she came home to New York. Only here did she feel a need to reconcile those old yearnings, the ones she'd held for him for so long, to prove to herself that the stupid mistakes she'd made had meaning. That the place of importance he'd once held in her life was not only genuine but also worthwhile.

People could say what they would about teachers and students. Despite her having thought she loved him—and the mess in her life it had made—what counted, what she continued to value, was his mentorship during her last semester in college. A witty note left on her studio door, a fifteen-minute conversation about Saul Steinberg, the electricity of immediate understanding. A connection that helped move her work forward, in both paint and clay. And if confusing learning with love seemed a tired trope, if Richard had already been sleeping with Lena, surprising everyone by eventually marrying her, Rachel tended to doubt she'd have graduated without his support.

She hadn't turned out to be the kind of fine-art painter he was, but every now and then Richard's encouragement still played like a distant tune in the back of her mind as she dipped the fine tip of a sable brush into a bright pool of gouache or drew a script-like stroke across a sheet of Canson paper. There would always be the sharp pang of moments she felt left behind, the confusion of sex, love, and art, a puzzle whose pieces she could never properly assemble. Painfully familiar shapes never quite fitting where it looked like they belonged.

Rachel would live her life without marrying or having kids, loving many without falling in love—not fully. Something was always held back, yearning like a persistent itch that wouldn't go away. She couldn't bring herself to want what was on offer, could only long for what was not, simultaneously believing she'd never get what she wanted, and that one day—one day—she would.

Richard would've liked to hug her but didn't—that greeting tacitly cut from their repertoire. Instead, with a faux flourish of gallantry, he pulled out a chair. Rachel laughed, bent as if in a curtsy, and sat down, both of them cringing at the sharp scrape of her chair legs against the tile. Richard was aware of the upper bridge in his mouth, replacing the front teeth knocked out in a motorcycle accident a decade before. The bridge had never posed a problem until this morning, when the gum felt sore, the fit not quite right, Sabine, his two-year-old daughter, headbutting his leg as he took it out and tried again. He was old, too old for this, for a second family. But Lena had wanted a baby, and he loved and coddled Sabine, spending more time with her than he ever had with his now grown-up kids, a son and a daughter whom—by their choice—he rarely saw.

"Everything okay?" Rachel said.

"Yes," he said. "Yes—it's good to see you."

"Lena?"

"Good too."

"And your girl . . . sorry—"

"Sabine. A handful." Richard ignored the impulse to take Rachel's hand, both embarrassed and touched by her ability to home in on his thoughts. And just like that, he blurted out his feelings. Remorse over that long-ago evening—the only one they'd ever have—and how grateful he was they'd been able to resume their friendship.

"I was so nervous," he said, but she just stared at him, her chin drawn back, her eyes open wide. "I mean, I—" he stuttered and glanced around, lowering his voice to add, "I'm much better than . . . you know." The look he gave her was a plea for understanding.

She glanced toward the counter, then down at his cup. "Anything left in there?"

"Help yourself," he said, a gulf of new regret opening in his chest as she raised the cup to her lips, took a tentative sip.

"Yech. Cold. How long have you been here?"

"Not that long."

"I was nervous too, you know."

"I do."

She seemed to consider then dismiss what she wanted to say until a tight-lipped frown worked its way into a smirk. "A poor choice of words." Again, she looked toward the counter, and he started to think she might leave. "I'm gonna get a coffee, but let me get this straight. You want to apologize for the . . . the quality?"

He nodded. What an idiot he was.

"The quality," she went on, "of the sex we had once . . . six? Is it seven years ago now?"

Sound carried in the glass-walled café, and a woman glanced over from a nearby table.

"Something like that."

"Well."

Richard braced himself, but her gaze, when he dared to meet it, was tinged with mirth, and relief swept through him.

"A bit of a travesty," said Rachel, "no?"

He could've told her he loved her then, and in the moment he would've meant it. But heightening the ephemeral sweetness of the times they'd met across the years—the sheer pleasure of those conversations and meandering walks, the lingering spark of attraction that hung between them—was the truth. When he was still a visiting artist at NYU—long-separated from but still technically married to his first wife—when he'd just begun what seemed merely another affair with Lena, who was already engaged to someone her age, it was as though he'd walked through a door that disappeared behind him. And his life, his real life, the one of painting and daily chores and settling into bed each night, would always be with Lena. Richard stood. "I'll get your coffee."

"A latte," she said, "and—"

"An apricot pastry," he said. "I know."

From Au Bon Pain, Rachel walked uptown along Lexington. It was warm for March, the light soft between the buildings with a promise of brightening, the kind of early spring day that brings the delight of dashing out for lunch without your coat. *The past is the past,* she'd told Richard. And that she, too, was just glad they still were friends.

Could she have lived with him in his tiny apartment downtown? In return for a child, could she have tended to his ego, his sexual and domestic needs, all the while making art, as Lena had, that seemed blatantly derivative of his? Rachel had always imagined Richard's attraction to Lena was a deep sexual connection, one strong enough to override the originality she'd told herself that Lena lacked. Sex between them *had* to be something fantastic, otherwise . . . what? Rachel tossed the paper cup with the dregs of her latte atop a wire container already brimming with garbage. Otherwise he'd have been with her? The sex they'd had was like the sex she'd had with boys in high school, brief and excluding, without a sensual or erotic note, and all the while she'd imagined it exposed a lack in her—an inability to come at such perfunctory mechanics. An absence of pleasure that made her betrayal of a boyfriend who'd always put her orgasms before his own all the more appalling. The sex she'd had with *him* had been easy and satisfying, if not wildly passionate. What was it she'd wanted?

At the light, the woman beside her touched her arm. "Are you all right?"

"Yes—why?"

"You're crying, dear."

Rachel swiped at each cheek. "I'm not."

AS IF | 2005

On the rooftop, Miguel cannot contain his rage. Forget the flight from L.A. and expensive hotel room, his elder son's court date left in the hands of his less-than-reliable ex-wife, the additional day off from work. Forget Lily's choice to spend the last afternoon of their weekend together at this Labor Day gathering of her old New York friends. That she's worn—no, saved—her sexiest dress for the occasion. But now Jackson? With his shaved head, his gym-enhanced arm draped across her shoulders, Lily along with everyone else rapt at his comic rendition of some loser's sad life—so much for client–therapist privacy. Miguel stubs his cigarette out on a curling shingle. This is why he's never gone in for therapy, though he's certainly been an ear for Lily's woes. Even if they've been his woes too—the unresolved death of her husband, Frank, Miguel's oldest friend and onetime partner in adolescent petty crimes.

Lily hadn't much cared for Miguel before. In return, he'd deemed her critical, overly intellectual, and chunky to boot, blaming her for how little he'd seen of Frank in recent years. But these last few months, in their common grief—memories, good and bad, shared in late-night calls—an undeniable attraction had grown between them, and he'd fallen, not in love, but into a romantic expectation, even the possibility, in time, of blending their families. Now his stomach roils with betrayal. Not just on his own behalf, but on Frank's. The pitch of her laughter, the shine in her eyes—clearly, she's in love with Jackson, his preference for men notwithstanding. Why she'd want them to meet is shameless, inexplicable.

Lily approaches him at the rooftop's edge, asks if he's having a good time.

Miguel can hardly look at her. "Hella good time," he says, letting acid bite into the words. "And you?"

Her expression sours, and it pleases him to see that he's hit the mark.

"If this is about my nightgown, I swear—"

"That schmanta you sleep in? No."

"It's *schmatta*," she says, her voice low and controlled, "and it's from Garnet Hill."

There'll be no recovery if he continues this way, but his mouth feels full of sawdust and, like the bad sister in a Grimms' fairy tale, only snakes and toads pour out. "You don't have any problem dressing for *him*."

Lily looks back toward the group surrounding the makeshift bar. "Who, Jackson?" At the mention of his name, Jackson turns his head, gives a little wave.

"Jesus," Miguel hisses. "How can you?"

"How can I what?"

Stomach it, he wants to say, but just shakes his head.

"No—tell me. I wanna know. Have you meet my friends? Not pay attention to you every second of every hour? We're in New York. It's a beautiful day. What are you, five?"

"It's fucking hot."

"You live in L.A."

"Did Frank know?"

"Oh my God—that I have friends who love me? Yeah. He did. He loved Jackson. I thought you would too. Did he know you were such an asshole?"

She's outdone him now, her shrill reproach silencing all other conversation.

"I'm going back to the hotel. Are you coming with me?"

"As if," she says, leaning into the words with the same derision as his check-kiting son.

"Suit yourself then."

Her voice cuts through his echoing footsteps in the empty stairwell. *"Oh, I will."*

Outside, on Seventh Avenue, cab after cab swerves past the corner where he stands, his arm held high, fingers tingling, crisp white shirt sticking to his back. A month before, at Lily's home down in North Carolina, Miguel had repaired the leaky taps of her bathtub and regrouted the tiles around them, had taken her and her two kids out to dinner at the best restaurant in town, flown back to California with an envelope containing photos of him and Frank from their teenage heyday. He could turn around. He could call her cell, plead the heat, jet lag, temporary insanity—ask her to please come down. But a cab screeches to a halt in front of him and he gets in.

"Where you going?" the driver says, the final "g" overly pronounced.

Miguel meets his gaze in the rearview mirror. "Beats the crap out of me."

PART TWO
EMMA

HOUSE-SITTING | 1982

In less than a week, Emma will have no place to live. Her thoughts keep turning to the one-bedroom walk-up she'd shared with Dennis for nearly two years. Dirty dishes stacked so high in the sink they bought paper plates. Late-afternoon sunlight skimming the keys of their old upright piano, her Broadway sheet music and his Beatles and Motown songbooks piled together on top. Just as she thought him the man she should marry after all, Dennis tearfully confessed that he loved her, but more like a brother—this when he had two sisters to boot. She moved her stuff into storage, slept on the couch of a friend whose generosity quickly faded into irritation. So began Emma's nearly six months of serial house-sitting.

She steps to the edge of the subway platform and stares into the dark tunnel, willing the train to appear. Once can be forgiven, but the director will not be pleased if she's late for rehearsal a second time. She can't imagine letting a total stranger stay in any apartment of her own, but other people are thrilled to have her stay. She's good at tending to things—as long as the things don't belong to her.

"Maybe you should get a job," says Emma's sister, Elaine.

Emma shoulders the phone to her ear, lifts the plastic hood on a tank of luridly colored fish, and taps in flakes of TetraMin ProCare, already regretting the moment of weakness that led her to call. In college, Elaine had been in plays too. Then she went to law school, made junior partner at a small firm in DC, and met Dave—the opposing counsel on a drawn-out insurance dispute who's now her fiancé. Their love and the lawsuit, they too cutely say, were settled out of court.

"I *have* a job," Emma says.

"I mean a real job, five days a week, like everybody else. Are they even paying you for this travesty in Brooklyn? What do they call that? Off-off-off Off-Off Broadway?"

"Not a lot, but yes. And it's not a travesty—it's . . . historically relevant," Emma says, quoting the promotional poster. Each cast member has been given a stack of them to distribute to small businesses for displaying in their windows. "This play could go somewhere—you don't know."

"Speaking of going somewhere . . . where you staying these days? You should have fought for that apartment, even if you weren't willing to fight for Dennis. Dave thinks so too."

"Oh, well—if Dave thinks so."

"Look, Em, you could always come down here and stay with us."

Emma counts the angelfish, which the owner has warned her have a propensity for eating each other. One of them is missing part of a fin. "You can't fight for someone who doesn't love you anymore."

The next morning, Emma sits at the kitchen island skimming the casting notices in *Backstage*. She'll read them more closely on the ride to Brooklyn. Right now she's wooing good juju with her nonchalance: parts or apartments—it's all the same. She walks the rooms, checking for any remnants of her stay, and rolls her suitcase to the door. Then she picks up the phone and dials.

"Actors' Service, this is Scott, how may I direct your call?"

"Scottie—hey. Emma Carlson, checking in."

"How's it going, Hollywood?"

"It's been better."

"Amen to that," he says. "Let me take a look. I've got a couple for ya. Let's see . . . your sister says call her at work 'if that's not too much to ask.' And Helen from the restaurant. Wants you to call right away. Emma, Emma, Emma . . ."

"I know, I know. The Actors' Service is for professional calls. Other messaging services can be made available for an additional fee. But I'm between places and—"

"Bravo. Maybe you'd like to work here. You're a smart girl," Scott says, then lowers his voice. "Tell your friends and family to at least make something up."

"I will. And thank you—thanks for not ratting me out."

"Don't thank me yet. I've got a slip here says your account is overdue."

Emma hangs up and dials Helen's number. Helen is thin and naturally blonde, with perfect teeth and a string of boyfriends. She's been in a Dentyne commercial and is an occasional day-player on *General Hospital.* Emma's looks have cast her as an immigrant extra in the movie *Ragtime*, plus her current role as a Polish peasant in the play, but not much else.

"Peasants-R-Us," she says when Helen finally answers. "You called about a sickle?"

"M-squared! Not a moment too soon. Tonight. You're working for me, yes?"

"Tonight?"

"Alec booked a room at the Helmsley Hotel for our one-month anniversary—so don't tell me no."

"Shit," Emma says.

"You're jealous, right?"

"I've got rewrites in Brooklyn till four."

"Just get there by five, and I'll work it out with Leon—he's the one who told me to give you a call. He says you're still homeless, so I figured—"

"Leon said I was homeless?"

"House-sitting—or whatever you call it."

Emma admits she needs a place, and Helen says she'll leave her keys at the restaurant if Emma will feed the cat, just for the one night. It's a studio apartment.

When Emma enters the church with her suitcase in tow, the cast is seated quietly in the first couple of pews. The director paces before the lip of the stage, reading aloud from a folded newspaper, his excitement palpable, though Emma's too far back to make out his words. Adam, the jingle singer who plays Emma's peasant husband, signals from the second row that he's saved her a seat. Emma tucks her suitcase into a back row, goes down front, and slips in beside him.

"Taking your act on the road?" he whispers.

"Tell you later," she whispers back. "Did we get reviewed?"

"Shush. He's just coming to the good part."

The director glances up and then continues reading. "As the ill-fated Rosa Luxemburg, the luminous Ann Marie Meadows is a standout in this ensemble piece, the skillfully sung harmonies of the chorus bolstering her pathos and exquisitely rendering the composer's haunting melodies of hope and despair. A surprising piece of theater, the trip to Brooklyn notwithstanding."

"I'd like to bolster his pathos," Adam says over the echoing whistles and applause. "There's only six of us—they couldn't mention our names?"

"Standouts notwithstanding," Emma says.

"Aw, you see? That's why I love you." Hugging her shoulders, he kisses the top of her head.

"Get a room," says Eli, from the pew behind them. He's also playing a peasant, and like Adam, he's already in rehearsal for another show.

"Get an agent," Adam says.

"All right, all right," the director calls out. "Let's warm up and take it from the scene where the luminous Miss Meadows gets shot."

Emma rises from the pew, but Eli asks her to hold up.

"Holding," she says, letting Adam and the rest of their row funnel past.

Eli says, "You know he has a girlfriend, right?"

Emma had been interested in Eli, but once she was cast opposite Adam, Eli shut her out. To be with either of them would diminish the brightness of whatever talent she's got, so blazing are their egos, but she can't deny their appeal, or her wish to put someone—anyone—between her and Dennis.

"I do know," she says. "Not that it matters, since there's nothing going on."

"Not for Adam, anyway—he just likes—"

"Don't take this the wrong way, but fuck off, Eli, okay? I can take care of myself."

"Really," he says.

"Meaning what?"

"Meaning this is the third time I've seen you bring a suitcase to rehearsal. I wouldn't have—" Eli pauses. "This isn't going very well. Can I start over?"

"No."

"You're not even curious?"

"About what?"

"About what I wanted to talk to you about."

"That's a lot of abouts," she says, and grins.

"I'm going on tour at the end of the run. If you're still stuck for a place to stay, you could—"

"Right, okay. That was it? Because, for a minute I thought—no, of course not. Ha. You need a house-sitter, I'm your man. Pets? Plants? Whaddya got? I have sensational references."

"That's the thing. I already have a subletter—a woman from my scene-study class—"

"Then that's just cruel," she says.

"Wait. I'm just trying to tell you that between the end of the run and the first of the month, my place will be empty."

"A couple of days, a couple of weeks from now—I got it."

"It's not much, I'll grant you. I just thought . . ."

Emma looks toward the stage. "If I needed," she says. "I know. Look, Eli, I . . . I'll see where I land."

At the restaurant, the booths are packed with teenage kids. By way of greeting, Leon holds up a roll of quarters, then cracks them open on the register drawer.

"Who are all these kids?" Emma says.

"Community Center Drama Club. Bet you can't guess what musical they're doing this year."

"*West Side Story?*"

"That's my girl," Leon says, handing her an apron and Helen's key. "Sharks up front in Tina's section, Jets in yours. I'll put that in the office," he says of her suitcase. "Better get out there. You doing okay?"

Emma wraps the apron around her waist. "Good as gravy," she says, picking up a pad of checks, just as Tina swings past her toward the kitchen window and slides an order across.

"That's the last of it," Tina says. "You missed most of the fun."

"Helen said it would be slow."

"Oh, it will be." Tina pours herself a Tab and takes a long drink. "We'll have the rest of the evening to clean up this mess. Busboy called in sick."

After the acne crowd clears out, the booths fill once at the dinner hour and then empty again. By nine, Emma's finished crossword puzzles in the *Times*, the *Post*, and the *Daily News*. She's almost done refilling the salt and pepper shakers when Leon seats a couple in Tina's section, even though it's Emma's turn. The woman is striking: sleek black hair bluntly cut to curve along the line of her jaw, her lipstick a confident dark red, her eyes glamorous with liner and smoky shadow. The man, bending down to retrieve a fallen fork, has dropped from sight. Leon slides into Emma's booth.

"Last thing you need, huh?" he says.

"What—another table? Yeah—I'm just here for the two-dollar wage."

The man in Tina's section straightens up, and it's Dennis.

"How many times has he been here?" Emma says.

"Coupla times, but never with a girl."

"And you failed to mention this, why?"

"You're hardly here, Em—what are the odds?"

She walks around to Dennis's table, determined to say something smooth, but the best she can muster is, "They don't have restaurants on the Upper East Side?"

His date looks up from her menu, first at Emma, then at Dennis.

"We were at the Loews on Broadway," he says. "I didn't think you'd—"

"Be here on a Monday night—no, neither did I."

Tina arrives with water and a basket of bread. "Problem?" she says.

"Hey, Tina," Emma says, in a parody of welcoming guests to a party. "This is Dennis—Dennis and . . . ?"

"Audrey," the woman says. "And you are?"

"Emma," he says. "This is Emma."

Audrey closes her menu. "You brought me to the restaurant where your ex-girlfriend works."

"Oh, it's not about me," Emma says, swiping her hand in the air. "It's the turkey club."

"Audrey—please," Dennis says. "We can go somewhere else."

"I would," Tina says.

"No, really," says Emma. "You should stay."

"Why don't you give us a minute," Audrey says, the words directed solely at Tina.

"Take all the time you like," Tina says, pulling Emma toward the kitchen. "We're not going anywhere."

A few minutes later, Dennis waves Tina over, places their order to go. While Leon rings them up, Emma takes refuge by the dishwasher's station.

"*Qué quieres, mi amor?*" the dishwasher says. "You need something?"

"*Necesito,*" she begins, as if with her smattering of Spanish she could tell him all she needs. The dishwasher runs a spray of hot water into a large sauté pan. There are sweat stains at the armpits of his T-shirt, and the skin on his hands is red and raw—he probably sends half his paycheck to family back home in Guatemala. Emma's breath is uneven, her heart still working too hard. "*Nada—gracias*," she says, finally. "Just . . . taking a break."

The last half hour, a few more customers straggle in: pie and ice cream for Tina, a couple of cheeseburgers for Emma. While their customers finish eating, Tina and Emma sit at the counter to add up their tips and exchange their coins for bills.

"Seventeen dollars," Emma says.

"At least we don't have to tip out a busboy," says Tina. "I've got thirty-two, but only because of the drama brats and your ex, who left a ten on the table—I should really give that to you."

"This isn't good," Leon says, staring past them toward the restaurant's entrance.

"No kidding," Emma says. "It's not even cab fare to Helen's. I'll have to drag my suitcase back on the train."

"Whatever happens," Leon says, "just keep your mouths shut." And without looking down, he drags his forearm across the counter, sweeping their bills and change into the bus tub below.

"What the fuck?" Tina says.

Emma swivels on her stool, following Leon's gaze. "Please tell me this is a joke."

"Shut up," he says under his breath. Then he opens the register drawer and steps out from behind the counter.

Emma glances over at their last customers, sunk into the cushioned booths and unaware of the two men ambling forward in nylon jackets and ski masks.

"No trouble," Leon says, holding his hands up at waist level.

"You got that right," the taller man says, and nods to his partner. "Let's do this thing."

The partner holds a gun up in the air for everyone to see, his steps almost dancelike as he moves past the booths and tables and kicks through the door to the kitchen.

"Ladies and gentlemen," the taller man announces. "If you'll kindly form a line up here by me, this won't take but a few minutes of your time."

His voice seems to bounce off the tile: resonant, with a wry authority that makes Emma think he could just as easily be doing voice-overs for car commercials as holding them up. She turns to Tina, but Tina's already joined their customers—strangers, looking unsurely back and forth at one another. Emma looks back at Leon. Suddenly she feels tired, like her legs won't move. He takes a step toward her, and the robber slams a hand into his chest and says, "You stick with me."

Emma gets in line behind Tina, and the cook and the dishwasher file out from the kitchen, followed by the gunman.

"That everyone?" the taller man says, pushing Leon slightly.

Leon nods.

"Good. That's good. We got an understanding." He tips his head toward the register. "There a deposit bag under there?"

Leon nods again and digs it out from the shelves below.

"Everything in the tray and under. Then my partner's gonna bring these nice people to the back while you open that safe in the office—you with me now?"

Leon hesitates.

"You with me?"

"I don't know the combination," Leon says.

The man only laughs and turns to his partner. "I love that story—don't you love that story? C'mon," he says, and takes the gun. "Let's go."

With Leon pushed out ahead of him and his partner taking up the back of the line, the tall man leads them all through the kitchen to a large closet where the linens are stored. He pulls the string for the lightbulb and motions them in.

Pressed behind their customers, their backs against the shelves of bar towels and pink liquid soap, Emma feels the heat of Tina's breath on her ear.

"Is this the part of the movie where we get killed?" she says, low enough for only Emma to hear.

Emma turns her face into Tina's hair and can smell the sweat of her scalp under the perfume of Herbal Essence. "One gun," she breathes back. "And that door doesn't lock. And Leon . . ."

When she doesn't go on, Tina leans just far enough away to look at her.

Emma shakes her head. No one would care about the hundred dollars in the register, but God only knows how much is in the safe—God and whoever tipped these guys off. Emma pictures her suitcase covered in Leon's blood—understanding, even as she sees it, that the image is a fantasy, a wish for drama, for something—anything—to happen. Leon will or won't do something stupid while she stands here helplessly in a linen closet, feeling sorry for herself. And after that? After the robbery, after the police reports, after a night at Helen's with the cat—after tonight will come tomorrow morning, and she'll still need to find a place to live. Not a house-sit, but a real apartment. If she ever gets out of this closet, she's going to call Elaine. Maybe borrow the money for a deposit.

Tina pinches her. "And Leon what?"

Emma unties her apron and wads it into a ball. "Leon knows the combination."

ALL THE WORLD IS NOT A STAGE | 1982

1. Emma

"What is *wrong* with you?" A woman's voice, ringing out from the midmorning street below. Over and over came the words, pitch and volume rising enough to make Emma wonder if she should dial 911. Peering out from Tina's West Side apartment, Emma saw a young white woman, like herself except for the pair of fuzzy pink slippers and the scanty floral robe clutched closed at her chest, as she crowded a man trying to get into his car. The woman pounded on the roof of the car, exhaust spewing as the engine turned over. "What is *wrong* with you?" she screamed, her voice tipping into a range only dogs could hear as the car pulled out into the street. *Yeah*, thought Emma in the silence that followed, *good luck with that.* But she was relieved—last thing she wanted was to spend another minute of her life talking to the police, who'd treated her and Tina like suspects the week before, when two masked men had held up the restaurant where they worked waiting tables.

It had been dark when Tina left for her shift, and Emma had pretended she was still asleep—hardly an actor's tour de force. Whatever this was, it was unlikely to last. If nothing else, it fulfilled her wish of putting someone between her and Dennis; wouldn't he be surprised. On the night of the holdup, he'd showed up at the restaurant with a date—a date! Harbinger of the trouble to come. What bothered her now, as the no-longer-screaming woman shuffled into a brownstone across the street, was not that her ex-boyfriend had been coming into the restaurant on nights he presumed she'd be off, but that no one, not even Leon, the night manager and she'd thought her friend, had the guts to tell her. Leon alive, but still in critical care, after several refusals to give up the combination to the office safe. A futile display of machismo she'd heard but not seen, having been backed into a linen closet with Tina and the half dozen customers left in the restaurant on a slow night at the end of the Labor Day weekend. All of them able to hear but helpless to stop Leon from being knocked about—sounds that, like the woman's shrill question, kept bouncing around in her head.

Emma had not enjoyed having to explain to the cops why her rolling suitcase was in the office. *Between apartments*, she'd said, earning her a skeptical glance and an unwanted note in the flipbook pad of the questioning detective. It grieved her to think that the nighttime busboy might've tipped the robbers off. A sweet-faced and overweight Puerto Rican kid from the neighborhood, improbably named Ivan, from whom they'd all bought their share of weed. He was meant to be there but had called in sick at the last minute. You didn't have to be a racist to connect those dots, but doing so left her with a feeling of self-disgust just the same.

What is wrong with you? her sister, Elaine, had said of Emma's decision to stay in New York, to keep working at the restaurant. For one thing, there was her part in the chorus of an avant-garde play, with its complex score and serious feminist message. And for another, there was Tina, offering to share her bed and her cozy place for as long as Emma needed, which was either a step up or down from the solitary house-sitting she'd been doing since Dennis told her he wasn't in love with her anymore. Rarely working nights, Tina had never met him, though he and Emma had been together for almost two years. *What a dick*, Tina had muttered, packing up his and his date's order to go. But it wasn't true. Dennis had tried to make her happy; it was her own ambivalence that had worn him down. A guy with a terrible weakness for a good turkey club.

"What is wrong with you," she said out loud, her breath fogging the glass.

Though she'd done little all day, Emma was late getting to work. At the restaurant, she reflexively pulled back from Tina's kiss.

"Well hello to you too," Tina said.

"Sorry—it's just here . . ." She raised her hand in greeting to the busboy who'd taken Ivan's place, wondering, for the briefest moment, how she would find another source of the mild weed she kept on reserve for extended bouts of insomnia.

"Oh, *here*," Tina said, drawing out the word. "Fucking straight girls. I gotta cash out."

"*Wait*." Emma grabbed the tie at the waist of Tina's apron. "Can we start again?"

"Who says we've started?"

"Just c'mere." Emma pulled her in close, kissed her full on the lips.

"So you do have some acting talent, then, don't you."

Emma usually enjoyed the sharp edge of Tina's banter, but that one hurt.

"Don't worry," Tina said. "I'm not kicking you out. You should maybe sleep on the couch, though."

"*Tina*."

"I'll leave some blankets out. Have a good shift."

"I don't get it—what'd I do?"

"You flinched, Em. You flinched."

"I didn't mean to."

Tina touched Emma's cheek. "Extra Brownie points for you then."

"Great. Just great," Emma said, tying on her own apron, in the aisle between the dishwashing station and the kitchen.

"You shouldn't fuck Tina," said the chef, whose temper and Moroccan chicken were equally renowned.

"*Excuse me?*"

"Shouldn't. Fuck. With. Tina," he said. "Are you deaf, now?" He raised the tip of the seven-inch chef's knife he'd been whipping through a pile of carrots, pointed it perilously close to his ear.

"Is it true you once threatened Leon with that thing?"

He grinned. "Could be. He gets on top of my skin."

"Under, you mean."

"I mean Tina, one time I cross her? Doesn't speak to me for a month. Just *toast please* and *order in*. Acts tough"—he held the blade flat to his chest—"but a tender heart."

"Did she say something to you?"

"I have eyes," he said, and went back to chopping.

Emma took a fresh book of checks from the stack by the soda machine and tucked it into her apron. "Can you make a burger for me?"

He smiled but didn't look up. "No chance."

"Night, chef," said Tina, sweeping past Emma with her bag and coat.

"Night, sweetheart."

Emma stared at him until he met her gaze.

"A whole month," he said, then tipped his chin toward the front of the house. "Better get to work."

2. Tina

Tina washed the dishes Emma had left in the sink, stripped the bed, and ran the sheets and her duvet through the basement laundry. Unable to fight the impulse, she refolded a warm blanket and a lighter summer quilt into a tidy stack, smoothed her hand across the freshly cased pillow she set on top. What she would've done for any houseguest, she told herself. It helped her simmer down. *Shit*, she said of the sun, now sinking toward the West Side Highway, the Hudson River beyond. Determined to wipe out the traces of a week's lapse in judgment, she hadn't stopped to eat. That fucking robbery. She would've liked to plunk down on the sofa, to rest her head on that welcoming pile, but if she raced and got lucky with the train, she could still get in to see Leon.

At the hospital, she had to wait in the hall, while the nurse helped Leon into the bathroom and returned him to the bed. There was always that squeak of rubber on linoleum, the rattling of gurney wheels, the stray laughter of staff on their way to the cafeteria. No use in observing any of these things, and yet Tina did. Unlike every other damn waiter at the restaurant, she wasn't an actor or an artist of some kind. But she was the only one who'd apparently given any thought to Leon, let alone paid him a visit.

"You can go in now," said the nurse, "but visiting hours are up in fifteen minutes."

"I know," Tina snapped, meriting a sharp look from the nurse. "Sorry—it's been a long day."

"Hasn't it, though," the nurse said, patting Tina's shoulder before moving past her and down the hall. Tina watched her walk away, her hand tracing the rail on the wall as if marking a familiar rhythm. Tina would like to be the one this nurse came home to. Her chunky white shoes kicked off at the door, the day's scrubs tossed into the wicker hamper Tina bought on sale from a fancy home furnishings store on Third Avenue. The nurse shimmying into a long sleep shirt before joining her on the bed, where they'd debate their favorite daughter in *One Day at a Time*, sharing containers of takeout Chinese, or maybe the pork chops and plantains from La Caridad, later finding comfort and more when they slid beneath the covers. Instead of flaky Emma, going on and on about the cast and her tiny part in the chorus of an "important play," the intensity that Tina had been drawn to having quickly grown tiresome, and the so-called trauma they'd shared in the holdup, just that and nothing more. A frightening moment that had brought them into sweat-smelling proximity but would not play out into anything beyond the few nights they'd spent. The nurse, in Tina's fantasy, would not pull back from her kiss.

Tina tapped her palm against the doorjamb, pasted a smile on her face, and entered Leon's room.

The fondness in his slow smile of recognition disarmed her. "You're a right mess," she said. "What were you thinking?"

"T—after all this time?" With a small wincing sound, Leon shifted in the bed. "Do you not know that I own a share? A small one. But still."

"I do now." She wanted to adjust the pillows for him, but it seemed too intimate a gesture. It was one thing to berate him in her usual style, another to potentially humiliate him. "Did they?"

He closed his eyes and blew out a long breath. Tina scooted the hulking hospital chair a little closer, scanned the IV drip line, then the scribbled erasable notes on a small whiteboard on the wall, but she couldn't make out the nurse's name. She'd just sit here quietly with Leon—she could do that. It's what she'd want.

"Not much of a detective, are you." Leon brought the heel of one hand to his temple, his eyes open now but focused on the ceiling. "Tina, Tina, Tina. You were there. Guy with the gun sure was sure I knew what was what."

The white of his left eye was filled with a bright clot of blood, the cheek below it still swollen and bruised. "You look like a boxer," she said.

"I'll take that as a compliment." He tugged at the gown where it was tied at his neck. "Fucking thing is scratchy."

"You want water?" Tina half stood. "I could ask the nurse for some ice."

"Oh, the nurse," Leon scoffed.

"What?"

"I may be hurting, T, but I'm not dead." He patted around the bed rail for the remote. "Can you raise this thing up for me? Just a little."

The first button she hit raised the mattress up under his knees; the next raised the whole bed up from the floor. Leon cleared his throat.

"Shut up, shut up—I got it." Tina sat back down, a hunger headache coming on.

"Could've been anyone," Leon said. "Didn't have to be Ivan."

"That's what I said."

"He's a good kid."

"I know."

"He came to see me."

Tina waited, but he didn't go on. "And?"

"And that's it. Could've been Ivan, but I don't think it was. He still quit, though."

"Why would he quit, if he wasn't involved?"

Leon turned his head and looked directly at her. "Because everyone assumes that he was."

Rather than returning to her apartment, Tina headed downtown, the subway doors briefly opening at each local stop and sliding closed again like an accusation, all the way to Christopher Street.

"I've done a stupid thing," she said to Abby, the weeknight bartender at The Duchess.

"How's that?"

Abby gave the bar top a fresh wipe before setting down Tina's beer, a Rolling Rock she was fonder of for sentiment's sake than for its taste. On the jukebox, Silver Convention singing the monotonous throwback "Fly, Robin, Fly"—how had they made a hit from a mere six words? Tina leaned in to better make herself heard.

"I've fallen for someone I'm pretty sure is just using me."

"Well, you can just stop seeing her, can't you?"

"I could, if she didn't work where I do and wasn't staying at my place." Before Abby could comment, Tina held up her hand. "That's not even the stupid part. I'm not her first, but she's on the fence. Oh, and on the rebound."

Abby clinked a soda glass to Tina's raised beer. "The full court of stupid then. You could always come stay with me and Sherise."

Involved with but away from other people at the time, Tina and Abby had once ended a drunken night in the same bed at the shared weekend beach house of a mutual friend neither of them had kept up with. Mildly amused but deeply hungover the next day, they'd parted ways at the Third Avenue jitney stop with a jovial handshake that sealed their secret.

"What, and ruin our beautiful friendship?"

"Yeah," said Abby, "that *would* be a shame. And Sherise would probably have a fit. But my couch is always there for you if you need it."

"Someone in the doghouse?" said the bouncer, Marie, helping herself to a handful of pretzels as she passed.

"*Am* the doghouse," said Tina. "Not in it."

"Oof," said Marie.

"I believe the word you're looking for," said Abby, "is *woof*."

They all laughed, a tiny moment of shared levity, for which Tina was infinitely grateful.

3. Emma

Emma's shift had been slow and without incident. At this rate she'd never afford an apartment even if she were able to find one—not that she'd started to look. Which was the problem. She'd never had to look before; something had always come her way. She would pick up the paper, but the minute she turned to the rental pages, she'd be filled with dread. Not just over what was involved—applications and references and deposits and people who'd gotten there before her and given the super a bribe—but as though something terrible would happen. Maybe this was the shock from the holdup. Or maybe she was afraid to be alone in a place that she solely was responsible for. Before Dennis, she'd had roommates. College friends who'd moved on with careers and families, or left New York as Elaine wished she would do.

Tina's building was walking distance from the restaurant, but Emma blew some of her meager earnings on a cab. The thing that replayed most often in her head was not the voice of the masked man who'd so enjoyed waving that gun about, or being pressed so close to Tina in the linen closet—that part of the movie, as Tina would say, having been replaced by Emma's pressing up against her full, naked body in bed. No. The clip that ran over and over in her mind was Leon sweeping their tips off the counter into the bus tub below. A gesture so oddly noble it broke her heart. She should go see him in the hospital. Maybe tomorrow, before rehearsal.

"Ma'am?" the driver said.

"Yes?"

"You're here."

"Oh, right—sorry." Emma dug bills from the pocket of her jeans. "Someone should make decent money tonight."

"Say again, ma'am?"

"Nothing," she said, stuffing bills into the little plexiglass drawer. "Keep the change."

Takeout menus were scattered across the lobby floor of Tina's building. Emma gathered them up into a neat pile that, seeing no other option, she placed to one side of the bottom step, before trudging up the stairs. The stairwell was dimly lit, and the echoing scuff of her shoes on the marble tread was a little unnerving, but the elevator was creaky and old, with one of those caged doors that always seemed to stick, and Tina's apartment was only on the third floor.

Emma had added Tina's key to a ring grown heavy with keys to other people's apartments, its clattering loud when it slipped from her hand. Tears stung at her eyes; was there not one thing that could go right? It had been convenient to stay here with Tina, anyone could see that, and the relief that followed a shared moment of danger—that heightened experience of fearing for your life—easily led to a sexual connection, wherever your preference might otherwise lie. But Tina's abrupt turnabout left Emma with a hollow feeling and a burn of shame. She would slip into bed beside her, find a way to make it right, to hold onto whatever it was between them for as long as she could.

The bedroom door was open, but Tina wasn't inside. Her bed was made, and Emma had the sense that the whole apartment had been shaken out like a fresh tablecloth. Of course their few nights together hadn't meant anything. Wasn't that what people always said of intense affairs and sudden physical attractions? *It didn't mean anything.* Tina had her own life—they both did, and certainly Emma, if anyone, was the flake between them—but there was a last-things feeling to her tidying up, as though she were never coming back. It seemed un-Tina-like to be out this late when she'd have to work early the next day, but how much did Emma really know about her? Last year Paige, one of the other waitresses, had fallen out of a tree in Central Park. Turned out she'd been packing away a quart of vodka on a daily basis. Emma looked around for a note, but the perfectly folded stack of blankets on the couch was the clear and only message. She picked up the pillow, held it to her chest, then flung it across the room. She would have to find yet another place to stay, and fucking hell if she didn't already miss her.

4. Tina

Come morning, she'd be sorry, but for now Tina was pleasantly drunk. Not enough to be sick in the cab ride uptown, but enough to wonder if she hadn't made a mistake, hadn't lost her one chance with Abby, all those years ago. Why *had* they so easily agreed to hush and never repeat their indiscretion? At the door of her apartment, she struggled to fit the key into the lock, the handle seeming to spin of its own accord before the door swung wide. Emma. For a moment, she'd almost forgotten.

"Where were you?"

Tina aimed for the couch, where the stack of blankets remained untouched. Had she meant to make Emma worry? She had. Let *her* be the one waiting around.

"Are you drunk?"

"Are you?"

"You could've left a note. Everything is so neat . . . like you weren't coming back."

"Jesus, Emma. I cleaned up. People do that. This isn't some stupid play."

"I know that. I'll find another place, all right? Just give me a couple of days."

"Whatever." Tina sank back into the couch, no pleasure left of her buzz. When Emma left, her apartment would be clean but empty.

Emma brought her a glass of water. "Drink."

"I'm fine."

"Drink it anyway. I'll make you some toast."

"Don't bother." Tina waved her hand toward the bathroom. "Aspirin, please—in the medicine chest. And I'm not the one you should worry about."

"No?"

"I saw Leon today. Not looking so good."

"I thought I might go tomorrow."

"Sure you did."

"What's that supposed to mean?"

"Whatever you want it to. Let's not . . ." A wave of queasiness washed through her. "I'm just gonna lie down here for a sec."

"Don't do that."

"It's my fucking couch. I'll do what I want."

"C'mon," Emma said. "I'll help you into the bed."

"You sleep in the bed. I'm good right here."

"Tina."

It was like a sinkhole, Emma saying her name. Pavement slipping beneath her, drawing houses and trees into the abyss of sadness below. "Can you *please* just leave me alone?"

"All right, all right. I'll just get you your aspirin."

Tina shoved the quilt to the floor, flung the blanket half-open across her side, the pillow cool against her cheek. She closed her eyes, listened to Emma padding around. The faint click of the aspirin bottle against the side table, the deeper darkness when she turned off the light. Some fussing around in the bathroom, then a long settling silence. Tina thought of Leon all alone in his hospital bed, of his pointless bravery.

"Are you there, Em?"

"I'm here, T. I'm here."

"Go see him tomorrow, will you?"

"Leon? I will."

"Okay, then. Good night."

"Are you all right?"

"What do you think?"

Emma laughed. "Come to bed?"

"Not tonight," Tina said. "Not tonight."

SATURDAY, 2:30 A.M. | 1982

"You'll never guess who came into the bar tonight," her girlfriend says. Sherise hates this sort of gambit. If she'll never guess, why not just say? From the spin, and the too-casual way Abby tosses her jeans onto the chair, Sherise knows that whoever it was isn't going to make her happy.

"Who?"

"Tina."

"Lindsay's Tina?" says Sherise, as if she didn't know. Lindsay, once also a bartender at The Duchess, had drifted from their circle when she quit, and Tina thankfully with her. "What's she up to?"

"Not much. In love with a straight girl."

"Hence the bar."

Abby laughs. "Hence the bar."

Sherise has never confirmed it but is pretty sure something happened between Abby and Tina on a summer weekend she'd stayed in town to console her sister, whose tempestuous marriage was in its last painful throes. Almost everyone cheats eventually—and Abby, who's never tried anything more than a little weed, is nothing like her ex-brother-in-law, who, beyond the coke, couldn't keep it in his pants. Sherise decided, still believes it best, to keep her suspicion to herself. But if Tina comes around, if she reenters their daily lives, she won't be able to leave it be. "Whatever happened with her and Lindsay anyway?"

"Lindsay, I think. Couldn't commit."

"Where's she living now?"

"Lindsay?" Abby parts the closed blinds with two fingers and peers through. "Beautiful moon tonight." She bends the slats farther apart. "Guess it's clouded over. Boston, I think."

"I wish you wouldn't do that—you're gonna ruin those blinds." Sherise means Tina but doesn't press. What she really wishes is that Abby would bring herself and those long bare legs into bed. She sets her book on the nightstand, the first in a fantasy series that Abby loves but Sherise can't seem to get into. In the awful years of her adolescence, she'd submerged herself in fantasy books, hiding from the world and her preference for girls. Now she wants a book to move her deeply, not just provide a means of escape, preferring the realistic contemporary novels Abby categorizes as much too sad. Sherise folds back the blanket. "You coming in?"

"My hip's been bugging me. Think I'll take a bath. You weren't . . ."

"No, no—it's late," says Sherise, though she'd stayed up hoping. Opposing schedules have not been kind to their sex life. She pats the book. "I'd have been asleep if it weren't for Nellisande."

"You don't have to read it if you don't want to."

"No, no—I want to."

"I know it isn't your thing—"

"I'm reading the freaking book, okay?" She digs her nails into her palms so she won't say anything worse, like *I suppose Tina likes fantasy books*, though the words are practically in her mouth. She'd rather not fight, though she'd like to wipe that shiny look of infatuation off Abby's face. They've come to a treacherous point of habit, doldrums they will either move through or drift apart in. The last thing Sherise wants to do is start over. She, too, had been that girl at the bar, grateful for Abby's kind and sympathetic ear. *You always grow to hate the thing that first draws you*, her sister warned when Abby moved in, only months after she and Sherise started dating. Nearly everything that comes out of her sister's mouth is caustic; it doesn't mean anything. She's got good reason to be bitter, but maybe she's right.

Sherise stares at Abby, possibly the love of her life, half-eager, half-dreading to hear what she'll say. Maybe a fight—a real fight, instead of their low-grade bickering—would put the wind back in their sails. But Abby, moving toward the bathroom, maintains her bartender's calm.

"I don't have the bandwidth for this, Risey—whatever it is."

Four years together, and a goddamn fantasy book is gonna break them. Sherise turns onto her side, gives her pillow a couple of good whacks, and plunks her head down. "I'm going to sleep. You do what you want." She reaches for the nightstand lamp, nearly knocking it over. "And don't leave the wet bath mat on the fucking floor."

Sherise closes her eyes but can sense Abby standing there in the dark, her practical mind weighing future options. *I don't want to lose you*, thinks Sherise, willing Abby to hear her without having to say the words. In the book, Nellisande, a waif-like creature with hidden strengths, can move through the timeline, righting potential wrongs before they ever occur. But in their Chelsea apartment, Abby flicks on the bathroom light and shuts the door.

EMMA REDUX | 2012

The problem, all these years later, isn't that Emma can't find her. A few clicks lead to Tina and her wife—the bartender from The Duchess that she'd always liked. Proud parents of a now teenaged daughter who, according to the glut of Facebook videos and emoji-riddled comments, has a gift for dance. The problem is what would she say? That she misses Tina's taste in music and the loose-wristed way she'd swing her hand, her fingers animating rhythm and pattern of melody along with the records she played? That she *did* love her then, maybe loved her still, but had damned herself to a solitary life because her preference leaned too strongly toward men? That, in low moments like this one, she understood but didn't quite forgive her for moving on.

No one wanted to be your maybe-I-could, to sense the effort involved. Sex had to mesh, to be more than comfort or a kind of favor. At least to start—even if, over time, it wound up that way. But time, to Tina, had already been wasting, though looking back they were still so young, tumbling toward adulthoods inevitably layered with regret. Tina had loved her in a way Emma couldn't reciprocate, neither of them happy as more than friends, which they'd stayed for a while. That closeness fading as they moved into separate lives, geographical distance dimming and eventually tamping their connection out, Emma almost the last of her friends to still live in New York. Where else would she go? *Anywhere*, her sister insisted the last time they spoke, but Emma had neither the wish nor the will to start over. Elaine would never understand that complaining about things didn't mean you wanted—or would ever be ready—to let them go. She'd given up her aspirations—wasn't that enough?

Alongside Emma's laptop, on the drop-leaf table—one of only a few pieces of furniture to survive her many moves—sits the renewal form for her current lease, which includes a 5 percent increase on her already overpriced junior one-bedroom in Midtown East. A fifth-floor walk-up whose once decent light has been compromised by the glass monstrosity of an office building still under construction across the street.

The New York of her twenties—that city of her heart—no longer exists. Late-night steak and eggs at Ruskay's on the Upper West Side, crowding into Hurrah's to see The Specials for less than twenty bucks, riding all the way downtown to the Pink Tea Cup for a slice of peach pie. A time when she hadn't fully understood the temporary nature of most things in life. This was not news—even back then, they'd waxed poetic about Orange Julius, about the Azuma and the great shoe stores on Eighth Street that were all long gone. It was a badge of belonging, a proof of citizenship to walk down the street recalling the establishments that had been there before. And yet Emma had maintained a youthful belief in stability, in a permanence that didn't exist, that certain places and things, certain opportunities, would always be there. You couldn't be a ballerina or an Olympic athlete or a musical prodigy, but your future was pretty much open if you made a concerted effort. There always was, and would always be, a new day.

Some people manage to grow their early success, to springboard on their first connections, later crediting everyone who'd helped them along the way. But the grim, groundbreaking play in which Emma had portrayed a peasant, a tiny chorus part, had been the only real piece of theater she'd ever been in, the character roles in film she'd dreamed of never amounting to more than extra work. Stage fright wasn't a problem—she loved to be in that golden light. It was the bare fluorescent-lit rooms of auditions where her nerves would reign. Her throat would tighten till her voice was hoarse and unclearable. She'd remember her lines, but her brain would short-circuit in the introductory conversations, leaving an inept impression. Once, when asked if there was any additional contact information beyond the answering service listed on her résumé, she'd been unable to recall, with any certainty, her own telephone number.

For a minute—in an elegant pair of custom-tailored gray slacks with pale silvery threads running through the fabric, a soft-shouldered white linen shirt with the feminine touch of pearl buttons, and a pair of low pumps made from fuchsia suede—she'd felt she could rise. That she could transform herself into any character, become the actress people kept telling her she had the talent to be. She could be tenacious in a given moment but had lacked the fortitude to back it up. All the money she'd poured into headshots and classes and therapy, all the money she could have put toward . . . what? *A mortgage*, Elaine would say. But Emma had never wanted to be beholden to real estate; she'd wanted freedom to move and had gone nowhere. Which was funny, when she could see it that way, but less so when all she felt was a low-grade mourning for what she'd lost and hadn't attained. Brave at the beginning, but a coward midway into careers and relationships, never able to make up her mind what was worth fighting for and what wasn't. She'd just fought with herself, stuck in a mire between can and can't. Where was it that she'd bought those clothes? *Charivari*. Gone with all the rest of the places she'd worked and frequented on Columbus Avenue. There would never be another day—not like the ones that had passed her by.

Emma picks up a pen and signs.

PART THREE
NINA

SINGLE LENS REFLEX | 1986

The photo shoot is just one more thing Nina doesn't want to do, but she's only been here a couple of weeks, and no one says no to the daunting Reynaldo. She is trying to maintain a good attitude. The display department at Bloomingdale's! This is her dream job. Only it doesn't look as if she'll ever see the inside of a store window. The only time she leaves his prop-packed closet of an office is to pick up his dry cleaning. Or to deliver point-of-purchase postcards to the fragrance and cosmetic floor, where the salesgirls smile at her with derision: she's Reynaldo's lackey. Wouldn't she like to try a little blush?

The bulk of Nina's job is to badger the merchandise managers at all the branches, making sure their displays conform to the flagship store. *Have you hung the C-prints that I sent last week? Do you think you might get to them today? Because it's only a two-week promotion—yes, of course I appreciate that you're busy. I'm busy too!* Sometimes at this point they just hang up. She wonders if phone solicitors make more than $8.50 an hour. When Reynaldo finally breezes in at ten o'clock, he's wearing one of his long, draping scarves around his neck, which means his shingles are bothering him. Nina isn't sure what shingles are, only that they make Reynaldo even more of a prick than usual. He drops his prescription slip onto the cleared cabinet top that is her desk.

"You don't have to go now," he says, patting her shoulder as if he's just done her an enormous favor. "You can get it at lunch."

He settles himself down behind the faux-marble desk that takes up half the room, puts on his reading glasses, and flips through his calendar.

"So you spoke to Nick?" he asks.

"Nick?"

"What am I going to do with you, Nina? Nick—the photographer—Nick."

"Mick," Nina corrects him, instantly regretting it.

Reynaldo closes his eyes as though maybe when he opens them she'll have disappeared.

"Nick, Mick," he says. "Whatever. Well? Is he coming?"

Flirting with Nina over the phone, the photographer had promised to swing by the office at ten fifteen. The last thing she needs is for him not to show up.

"He should be here any minute."

"All right then, good," Reynaldo says, rearranging his scarf. "The guard, he will meet you this evening, at the Sixtieth Street entrance. Nine forty-five sharp. You remember—yes?"

Nina doesn't want to be locked inside an empty department store alone with some guy she doesn't even know—it makes her uneasy. And Reynaldo, knowing that she lives close by, is sending Nina home early this afternoon so he won't have to pay her any overtime. She'll help set up umbrellas and keep track of the film, and he won't have to pay the photographer for an assistant either, which hardly seems right. If the photos are so damn important, Nina wants to know, why won't Reynaldo be there? Although, if he's trusting her with the shoot, maybe she's making strides—better than the dry cleaners or the pharmacy.

"I want all the spring launch counters," Reynaldo says. "Are you listening, Nina? With special attention paid to Lancôme and Dior. And do not forget the central displays with the new factice."

There's no pleasure for her in the girly world of cosmetics and fragrances; Nina wears only the minimum required for her to fit in. But she loves the fantasy of the displays. The iridescent colors, the clever ideas, even Reynaldo's precious factice: the giant replicas of perfume bottles whose pale liquids delicately refract the light, ironically filled not with expensive fragrance but with solutions of alcohol or formaldehyde.

"If you screw this up," Reynaldo adds, "I will be very disappointed."

"Who's disappointed?" Mick says, leaning into the room. "We haven't started yet!"

He sets his portfolio down by Nina's chair, his left hand grazing her back as he steps forward, extending his right one to Reynaldo.

"Mr. Stevens," Reynaldo says. "A pleasure to see you again."

"Likewise. Please. Call me Mick."

"Nina," Reynaldo says, reaching for his wallet, "why don't you bring us some coffees?"

"I'll get this," Mick says, pulling a wad of singles from the front pocket of his jeans and pressing them firmly into Nina's hand.

"Two *cafés con leche*," he says, winking at Reynaldo, and then to Nina, "get yourself something too—a Danish, or whatever you like."

A Danish—what's that supposed to mean? That she looks hungry? God—she hates this job. The bills are warm in Nina's hand. How old is he, she wonders—maybe twenty-eight? Dark circles below his eyes, a subtle thickening of his waist under the pearl-snapped cowboy shirt—no, thirty-six—a little old for her. His skin is sallow, but the dark curly hair and boyish features still lend him a certain faded-rock-star charm. Nina senses something decrepit—a slightly acrid odor beneath his cologne—that does nothing to deter her attraction.

That evening, nine forty-five comes and goes as Nina waits for Mick at the appointed entrance. The guard smells of raw onion and old cigars, pokes his pinky fingernail around one of his incisors, and sucks his teeth. When Mick finally steps out of a cab, Domke bag slung across his shoulder, it's ten fifteen.

"Right on time!" he calls to Nina, then pulls strobe cases and a couple of stands from the trunk of the cab. "Hey, my friend," he says to the guard. "Could you give us a hand?"

With a smirk of amusement, the guard turns to Nina. "You got forty-five minutes. Better synchronize your watches."

"What the hell was his problem?" Mick says, once they're settled inside.

"We should get to work. Reynaldo wants you—"

"Don't you worry about Reynaldo. I've got this under control."

"No—I mean, right—I'm sure you do. It's just he—"

"Likes things a certain way?"

"Yes," says Nina. "He does."

Mick raises the tripod. "Come look at this. Just for the banners."

Through the lens, she sees a well-framed view of the central display, featuring the flower-bordered banners. *SPRING FLING!*

Mick squeezes her arm. "You shouldn't worry so much. And anyways, I brought us something to help move things along." From the pocket of his shirt, he pulls out a tiny folded envelope.

"You're shitting me," says Nina. Why are these people her problem?

"What? You don't partake?"

"No, it isn't that—I mean, Jesus, Mick. Give me a break."

"Hey, Neen—if Arthur Conan Doyle wrote Sherlock Holmes coked out of his mind, I think we can manage to take a couple of pictures for Mary Kay."

She's hard put to determine the most stupid—or least offensive—part of that sentence. He's even made her bristle on Reynaldo's behalf.

"It's Nina. And don't call him that."

Right there in plain view, Mick's already laying out lines on the Clinique counter with his American Express card. He looks up at her and grins.

"Sorry," he says. "Nina. Of course."

He snorts one line, and then another, leaving two on the glass, next to a tester for shadows.

"Would you look at all this crap?" He sweeps his hand toward the maze of counters done up in pastel colors. "It's like an Easter parade."

Suddenly Nina feels exhausted. Mick holds the rolled-up single out to her. She imagines the warm rise into the high, Mick's clothes on the floor of her bedroom, the feel of his lanky arms wrapped around her waist. It's been so long—who would she be hurting—who'd even know?

"Shit," she says, shaking her head. "Oh, what the hell."

Nina's only hoping for the warmth of another body, but later, at her apartment, Mick surprises her with an enthusiasm she isn't expecting after all the coke. He's brought his portfolio along as well, and after they've separated, both sticky with sweat, she asks to see it, even though she's convinced it will be a mistake. Which it is, only not the way she thinks.

"Don't look so shocked," Mick says, rubbing the last of the coke over his gums as she turns the pages.

"This is what you showed Reynaldo?"

"No, no—this is my personal work, not that commercial garbage."

The photos are a black-and-white series, portraits of kids on the cusp of adulthood—perched on subway platforms, the rims of fountains, peeling wooden benches in Central Park—their raw expressions of hope and sorrow bared before the lens. Nina can't put them together with the guy in her bed. In the empty department store, she'd thought him only reckless—his idiotic comments, his mediocre eye. Base attraction had done her in. Now she wonders, when he looks at her, what does he see?

"Why'd they let—" Nina puts her hand over her mouth, shakes her head, and starts again. "How'd you get so close?"

Mick shrugs. "I get around. Got anything to drink?"

"I'm sorry," Nina says.

Missing her meaning, he says, "Not even juice?"

She sets the portfolio aside and pulls him toward her.

"Yeah—okay, okay," Mick says, and laughs. "I like you too."

Despite the scarcity of shared personal details, it never crosses Nina's mind that he won't call her. A week passes, and Reynaldo wants to know where his photos are.

"He said it might take him a couple of days to get over to the lab," she says, thinking it plausible, though it isn't true. "I'm sure he'll call when they're ready."

"Yes, I am sure you are sure," Reynaldo says with unveiled disgust. He pushes Mick's business card to the edge of his desk. "But why not call him? Why not call him right now?"

She takes the card, pushes the numbers into the black plastic phone.

"Hello?" a woman screeches into her ear. In the background, Nina hears the wail of an infant. It sounds like the sadness of the whole world.

"Oh. Hi—hello. Is Mick available?"

"Is Mick available," the woman sneers. "Who is this? One of his fucking girlfriends?"

"No—I'm . . . sorry to bother you." Nina presses two fingers to her forehead. "This is Nina, from Bloomingdale's. Could you please just have him call Reynaldo?"

"Reynaldo—who's that? Your pimp?" The woman laughs, hysterical or drunk—it's hard for Nina to tell. As the baby's crying comes closer, she can hear Mick's voice.

"Stacey," he's saying. "Stacey, please. Gimme that phone, or I'll fucking kill you."

Nina hangs up and looks at Reynaldo.

"Well?" he says, staring her down.

"He wasn't," Nina falters. "He wasn't there."

Now he mimics her too.

"'Could you please just have him call Reynaldo?' No, Nina—that will not do. 'When do you expect him? It is of the utmost importance.' These are the things you must learn to say. I cannot be waiting for some idiot photographer to return my call. Do you understand?"

The dual ringing and blinking of his extension startles them both. Reynaldo holds up his hand, meaning both that he'll get it and that they'll finish this later.

"Reynaldo De Silva," he says into the phone. And then a few seconds later, "Excuse me?"

When he holds the phone away from his ear, Nina can hear the woman's voice. She hears the words "cunt" and "little whore" before Reynaldo hangs up.

"A delightful woman," he says, "this Mick Stevens's wife. She informs me that when hell freezes over I will get my 'fucking photos.'"

Over his half glasses with their gaudy chain, Reynaldo's tired brown eyes take Nina in. He shakes his head like some old abuela, and then he says, "Nina. What did you do?"

FALLOUT | 1988

Half an hour late for work, Nina holds up the blown inner tube of her front bicycle tire as she enters the studio.

"Second Avenue is lined with *nails*—I swear to God," she announces to the room at large. And then to Rob Angstrom, a photographer in his own right who's working as the assistant on this catalog shoot, she says, "What's with the pink shirt again, Angst? Didn't you go home last night?"

The nickname's ironic; square jawed and six foot three, he's possibly the best-looking and least anxious man she's ever known. And even though facetious rank-outs are the currency of affection on teams like this one, where they've all worked together many times before, Nina's dig falls into dead air. Elliot, the soft-goods stylist and her tantrum-throwing boss, holds half a cream cheese–smothered bagel inches from his mouth, which hangs open, dramatically aghast.

"*What*," she insists, "I can't make fun of him for getting laid?"

More puzzling to Nina than their stunned expressions is how they're all still grouped around the bagels and donuts instead of working. The photographer clears his throat.

"Angst's apartment burned down," he says.

"Yeah, right. And the dog ate my homework. Hey, did anyone ever really use that excuse?"

Only Angst looks amused. "The boiler," he says. "In my building. It blew up last night."

"*Noooo . . .*"

"Three-alarm fire. Made the ten o'clock news. *Hoboken blaze lights up the sky.* Don't you watch TV?"

"But your photos," Nina says.

"All gone. Everything's gone."

She giggles, saying, "Oh, my God." And then, "Seriously—Rob—I'm so sorry. I don't know why I'm laughing."

"'Cause you're a cold-hearted bitch?" Elliot offers.

"Well, *that.* And maybe the shock. All you have left is that stupid pink shirt?"

"The gear I had here in the studio, and *yes.* Just the clothes I'm wearing. My favorite, by the way, pink shirt."

Angst does a little fashion turn, and he and Nina crack up.

For what now seems like the first time in her life, Nina feels all right. Better than all right—she feels good, liquid good, shiny brilliant magic good—which she knows can't be good at all but is still denying that fact. Long past the lift the MAO inhibitor was meant to lend, she's moved on to another kind of ride, wooden tracks *click-click-clicking* as her car mounts the rails, traveling ever upward. Nina imagines Icarus on his glorious flight toward the sun—how the fading of the gray world below must have filled his heart with untempered joy.

At eleven the night before, while Angst's charred belongings were being doused by New Jersey firemen, Nina had ridden her bike from Fiftieth Street down to Washington Square, amazed again at how brightly lit the empty avenues were. She'd circled around and around the fountain as though on a carousel, occasionally nodding to one or another of the dealers who haunt the park's archaic wooden benches newly painted a forest green. Young men in the shadows, no longer surprised by her presence—this girl, her hair flowing in the polluted summer air, dipping in and out of the park on a French ten-speed racer. At first she'd worried someone would stop her, try to steal the bike, but she'd merely become a familiar part of their nighttime scene, the park her secret playground.

In bed at 2 a.m., when she was finally tired, Nina had savored the cool sensation of freshly laundered sheets against her skin; her apartment was easily cleaner than it had ever been before. *Astonishing*, she'd thought, drifting into a thin approximation of sleep, *what could be accomplished with all this energy, all this extra time*. And then, at five she'd woken abruptly thinking about Rob Angstrom. Had she sensed the fire? Known something was wrong without understanding? Loss seeping into her consciousness as dawn bled through the slats of her bedroom blinds? She feels fine-tuned to the world, the sensitivity that only pained her before transformed into thousands of golden threads that join her to everything. She loves her life, her job, the city—even Elliot, her impossible boss. Sometimes she feels a little dizzy, but that side effect—as the psychiatrist promised—is easily remedied by the cup of black coffee she now holds in her hand. She should probably tell him, or her chipper therapist, that she's barely been sleeping. Although, what's the harm when she's doing so well?

"Yo, space cadet," Elliot says.

"What? Oh." Nina doesn't know how long she's been standing there, musing over the ripples in the dark acidic brew that fills her blue-and-white paper cup, with its silly illustrations of amphora urns, the zigzagging marvel of its Greek key designs. Elliot indicates a pile of flowers beside the sink, white freesias and dozens of newspaper-wrapped roses in peachy shades that need to be snipped and put into water.

"Any time today," he says, and then tilts his head. "Are you okay?"

Nina raises her cup to him in a toast, quotes the words in the faux-Grecian font printed on its sides.

"We are happy to serve you."

Because of the fire, Angst is staying at his aunt's pied-à-terre in an elevator building right around the corner from Nina's fourth-floor walk-up. It's Friday, the last day of their shoot, and he's meeting her for breakfast at a neighborhood diner. When Angst slips punctually into the booth at seven thirty in a fresh set of clothes, Nina has already finished the *Times* crossword puzzle and two cups of coffee.

"My landlord's a criminal," he says. "It's a fucking miracle no one was hurt. Though," he adds, scanning the menu, "my upstairs neighbor claims her cat is suffering from smoke inhalation."

"That's it?"

"I didn't see it go up in flames. Just the drowned remains."

He doesn't offer, and Nina doesn't ask, where he was.

Their waiter approaches, holding his hand out to Angst. "So this is your friend?"

"Rob, this is Nikos, my favorite waiter. Nikos—Rob. And that's Stavros," she says, leaning forward and tipping her chin to the heavy-browed man in a tuxedo shirt waving a spatula from behind the counter.

"Blueberry muffin toasted on the griddle?" Nikos says to Nina.

"Yes, please."

Angst orders "the Athenian" special: three eggs sunny-side up, sausage links, potatoes, and whole wheat toast. Nikos nods approvingly, tears their order from his little pad, and hands it across the counter to the still-beaming Stavros.

When their food arrives, Angst studies her between mouthfuls of yolk-smeared toast. "Something's different about you," he says. "You're—I don't know . . . sexier or something—you've got a glow. You're not pregnant, are you?"

"Hardly," Nina says.

"Not seeing that drummer anymore?"

Fucking Elliot and his big fat mouth. Nina's sure she never told Angst about Lee. The Kentucky transplant with the husky voice, charming when he drank but then spiteful and withdrawn once he was sober, the rebound guy from the longtime boyfriend who'd broken her heart. Instead of cheering her up, he'd only made her more depressed, which had led to the therapist who'd suggested the psychiatrist with the miraculous meds. She should really call Lee and thank him—he'd done her a favor being such a crappy fling.

"Him? No," she says, tossing it off. "Why? What are you asking?"

"Nothing. We're friends. And I'm so close by. We should go for a drink."

"You and me."

"Yes, Nina. You and me—why's that so strange?"

"Well, for starters, I'm not a model."

"Ouch," he says. "So I like beautiful women. Doesn't mean I haven't noticed you underneath those baggy clothes."

Nikos stops by the table to refill their cups. "You like our girl?" he says to Angst. "She's beautiful, no?"

"I was just saying that very thing."

"Aw, Nikos just loves me 'cause I'm a big tipper."

Nikos laughs. "A little money never hurts," he says, laying down their bill. Angst takes the check, holds it out of Nina's reach.

"Oh, very fancy now," she says. "You're picking up the tab?"

"For coffee and a muffin that you barely touched? Yeah—I think I can afford that. So what do you say?"

"To what?"

"You're not going to make this easy, are you? To a drink. I've got to edit film right after work—but I'll be done by eight."

Nina thinks of all the jobs they've worked together, the crush that, knowing better, she's struggled to hold in check.

"Sure," she says. "What's the harm in a drink between friends?"

When Nina gets home from work, waiting on the shallow step at her building's entrance is her ex-fling, Lee. Forearms resting casually on his bony knees, blond streaks freshly bleached into the darker brown layers of his long feathered hair.

"What are you doing here?" she says.

"That's some fine hospitality you got going for you there," Lee says, reaching behind him. "I got you this."

Tucked into a miniature wicker basket with a blue gingham bow is a bouquet of silk pansies, which Nina finds equally heartrending and repulsive. She notes his backpack leaning against the wall.

"For your birthday," he says.

"Which was two months ago. But thanks, I guess. So what are you doing here, Lee? I thought you were back in Kentucky."

"Again with the third degree—dang, woman, that's cold. Came up to see Annie, who neglected to put the key under the mat before she took off for the whole goddamned weekend."

On summer weekends, Lee's sister Annie sells crystals and jewelry at the Renaissance fair in upstate New York. When Nina was dating Lee, he was living in the tiny second bedroom of Annie's apartment, in a crumbling tenement on the Lower East Side.

"She's still doing that?" Nina shakes her head. In a building where the front door doesn't lock, only his sister could leave a key under the mat and not get robbed. "What about Kevin? Can't you stay with him?" She couldn't care less about his sister but still misses Annie's flamboyant neighbor, Kevin—his lost affection part of the fallout of her messy breakup with Lee.

"He's the one who drove her up to that God-awful fair." Lee grins. "I'm getting the feeling you're not happy to see me. Stupid flowers, anymore—should've got you candy."

"Or, you know, called."

"Not nearly as romantic, I'd have to say. Look, Nina, I got nowhere to go. Show some mercy, babe, okay?"

"*Mercy?*" Nina has a sudden urge to slap him. Then she starts to laugh.

"I pour it on too thick?"

"Just a tad," she says, taking out her keys. "One night on the couch, Lee. That's it—I mean it."

"That's all I'm asking. Got any bourbon upstairs? You look good, by the way."

"Yeah, yeah. So I've heard."

Later that evening, as she gets ready to meet up with Angst, Lee trails her around the apartment saying, "Don't you worry about me!" which only makes Nina feel more uneasy about leaving him there alone. The air is tropical and oppressive when she steps outside. All she has is Angst's number at his burned-out apartment in New Jersey—now she's got to walk over to his aunt's apartment, where he's staying through the weekend, just to tell him that she can't go. Who knows what would have happened? Probably nothing, but Nina's annoyed and disappointed that she won't find out, and even more so to realize she must still have a soft spot for Lee. Why else wouldn't she just tell him to go to hell when he showed up on her doorstep?

Waiting for the light, Nina can see into the window of an empty apartment across the avenue. Or a room empty of furniture, at any rate, where a lean-bodied man in Lycra shorts is—*yes*—sitting on a trapeze. It's a fairy-tale image, the way he moves past the illuminated window, swinging back and forth. Nina smiles, breathes in, and sighs. It's so New York—that flash, the sudden fleeting view into a moment of ecstasy, private and yet open to the street for anyone to see.

Outside his aunt's building, Nina tries to explain her situation to Angst over the intercom, but he keeps interrupting by pressing the buzzer and saying, "Just come up."

When the elevator arrives at his floor, Angst, tall and beautiful as ever, leans in an open doorway down the hall.

"You're not getting away that easy," he says. Angst kisses her and then licks her lips. Nina laughs at the sensation of her knees weakening.

"Kind of early in the evening for a booty call," she says. "Not that I don't—God knows, I want to—but you . . . it's just . . ."

"Just what, puppet?" he says, pulling her closer.

"Just that we work together all the time. So, yeah. I don't think I should do this. Plus, I've got Kentucky at my apartment—"

"What's he going to do?" Angst says, smoothing his hand across her forehead and down her cheek. "Set the place on fire?"

Walking home from his aunt's hours later, Nina feels as though she's traveling in a foreign country. Looking over her shoulder, she counts up the stories to locate the apartment where Rob Angstrom now lies soundly asleep. A few buildings away, the other window, so brilliant earlier, is a dark, hollow cave, the trapeze artist gone—sleeping too, or maybe, as Nina dreamily imagines, drifting to the stars. At first she was deeply afraid that she'd made a mistake. The sex with Angst, though passionate, was rougher than she was used to; he'd bitten her breasts so hard she'd cried out in pain. But afterward, they'd lain side by side on the living room rug, talking about their lives and watching heat lightning flicker through the open blinds—a moment of intimate perfection she'd have sold her soul for.

After slogging up the four flights of stairs, Nina slips into her darkened apartment like an errant kid coming in after curfew. Lee, who's been sitting on the edge of her bed, switches on the night table lamp as she enters the room.

"It's three a.m., Nina," he says, quietly. "What the fuck are you doing?"

She shields her eyes. "What the fuck are you? Are you out of your mind? You scared the crap out of me."

"Naw—you're scaring me. Probably your neighbors too—might want to keep your voice down. So who is this guy, anyway? This *friend* you're out having drinks with till all hours of the morning?"

"Oh my God—like that's any of your business! Keep my voice down? What are you even doing here? What are you doing in my room?" Nina wipes her hand across her mouth; she feels ill, as if her organs are pressing out through her skin. "You should go—I really think you need to go."

"Go where? Where am I supposed to go? What about your little photographer friend? Maybe I can fuck off to his place—oh no, wait—that was *you*."

"Lee! Don't be such, don't be . . . *whoa*." Nina grabs the doorframe, slides her body to the floor.

"Hey, now," Lee says, standing up. "You . . ."

"What?" she says, closing her eyes.

"Don't take this the wrong way, but you are just . . . *sweating*, you know, like a pig."

"Yeah, that's helpful, thanks. Think you could get your Southern ass into the kitchen, get me a glass of water?"

The next morning, it takes a minute for her head to clear. Sleep. She'd just needed sleep. Nina smiles at the comforting smells of coffee and bacon. Maybe she'll eat. Lee always did make a good breakfast. And last night, once he'd snapped out of his idiotic tantrum, she'd been glad he was there to see her through her dizzy spell—or whatever it was. He'd tried to convince her to go to the ER, which she hadn't done but still found touching.

Nina is cautious getting out of the bed, but when she stands up, she feels perfectly fine. She stretches her arms, bends this way and that to test her balance: all systems go. She slips on yesterday's jeans and what she's surprised to find is her last clean T-shirt.

"You're up!" Lee says as she enters the kitchen. He turns the flame down under the pan. "Couple more minutes here till crispy. You feelin' okay?"

Nina pours herself a cup of coffee. "Actually, I feel pretty good."

"But you're still going to call the doctor, right?"

"Aw, you're still worried, Kentucky—that's sweet."

Lee lays out sheets of paper towel on a plate.

"I put your keys in that dish by the phone. And I took a twenty from your wallet—for the breakfast and such."

"Right. That's not so sweet."

Lee chuckles. "Guess nothing's changed, huh?"

"No," says Nina. "It hasn't."

It's only after Lee's gone that Nina realizes he's left her not only twenty dollars lighter but with a sink full of dirty dishes and bacon grease splattered everywhere. Plus, there's the distressing little basket of flowers, which she buries in the kitchen garbage beneath wet coffee grounds.

She calls the psychiatrist, as a matter of form, hanging up when her call goes to voicemail. Not that she expected he'd be there on a Saturday. Weeks ago his receptionist left a message on her machine, canceling her last appointment. Now every time Nina tries to reschedule, she gets his voicemail, where she dutifully leaves a message but never hears back. *Family crisis*, the receptionist had said. Meaning what? That she should worry about his problems too? *There's a* New Yorker *cartoon in there somewhere*, Nina thinks, laughing to herself. It doesn't matter; she feels fine, and she's got things to do, like laundry, for starters. Tomorrow she's working for Angst, on a wedding shoot, and she's got nothing left to wear.

Nina's at the Laundromat unloading her dryer when she notices that the smooth white surfaces of all the machines have an iridescent aura. She tries to dismiss this to the buzzing fluorescents, but her thoughts are harder to ignore. From the jumble of chaotic details floating through her mind, an epiphany is forming. *It doesn't matter if you fold your clothes, because none of this is real.* She places her hand on another dryer door. Behind the warm glass, the colorful clothes of a stranger spin and swirl in a stunning array. *Fold the clothes, don't fold the clothes—it's all illusion.* She can manage this trippy bleariness, even the Buddhist construct. It's the notion lurking in its wake that troubles her—the subtle suggestion that it might not matter if she were dead. Sitting down in a wobbly plastic chair, Nina allows for what she's known all along. The Nardil's not making her better; it's making her manic. She's not happy. What she is, is high.

On Sunday morning, it's still cool enough for Nina and Angst to drive with the windows rolled down. The wedding shoot is in Connecticut, and Nina's trying to memorize everything about the ride up. The lush woods along the highway, the brilliant blue vault of the cloudless summer sky, the tiny creases at the corners of Angst's warm brown eyes when he turns to her and smiles.

After the episode in the Laundromat, she'd called her therapist, confessing how little she's been eating and sleeping, that she's starting to feel like she's been dosed with LSD. Her therapist wanted her to get out of the shoot today, but Nina had refused—she's not flaking out on a job with Angst. At least she'll have one last day of princess-mania before all her coaches turn back into pumpkins. Once she's Cinderella again, she doubts he'll want her anymore. Not that she'd told her therapist that. Their conversation had been filled with Nina's accusations: Why hadn't the therapist noticed anything was wrong? How was the psychiatrist supposed to monitor her when he couldn't be bothered to keep his appointments or return her calls? If she stopped taking the meds cold turkey, her therapist warned, there'd be harmful effects. More arguing had followed, and finally her therapist called in a favor—a specialist over at Columbia. Nina agreed to see him Monday afternoon. Until then, she'd hang on in the fairy-tale heights, her descent, for the moment, delayed.

The wedding's at a sprawling mansion, with a wild English garden, belonging to the parents of the bride. Not having brought sunblock or even a hat, Nina's going to bake, her fair skin fry. She forgot he'd told her they'd be shooting outside. They've barely finished setting up when the guests begin to arrive, and for Nina the whole ceremony flies by in a series of reloaded film backs. She carefully seals the paper tabs and labels the rolls with her sweaty hands—it's all she can do to keep up. Maybe her therapist was right; more than anything she wants to lie down in a cool, quiet room. Now Angst is deftly moving people around for the formal group shots, and every time she has a chance to look up, the maid of honor or some other beautiful woman in a strapless dress is flirting with him. Nina feels weak from the heat and the pressure, and the helpless jealousy burning through her. Like a mantra, she repeats to herself: *At least the reception will be indoors.*

Once they've moved inside, she feels a little better. Over the crowd of lively guests, the bartender catches her eye. He makes an exaggerated gesture of wiping his brow and holds up a bottle of Perrier. Nina puts the Ziploc bag full of film into the camera bag on her shoulder and holds her palms together at her heart in gratitude. The bartender gives her a thumbs-up and then points her out to a passing waiter.

The flash of Angst's camera bounces around the room. Nina has a loaded back ready when he approaches, his Pentax held high. But instead of switching the back out, he takes the bag from her shoulder and, along with the camera, tucks it into one of the hard cases they've stashed in the corner.

"Dance with me," he says.

"What, now?"

"Relax," he says, nodding to the maid of honor, who wriggles her fingers as she dances past with the groom. "Miss Thing there's going to let me know when it's time to cut the cake. C'mon, Ginger Rogers, let's see what you got."

As Angst whirls her around the room, Nina meets with dirty looks from several of the female guests; a disdainful hatred has replaced the maid of honor's smile, reminding Nina of a popular girl in junior high who once pushed her to the ground.

"Nice wedding," Nina scoffs. "Did you see the look she gave me?"

"I see only you."

Nina knows it isn't true, but it thrills her to hear him say it. She lets her head rest on his chest, thinking, *All I need now is some glass slippers.*

Ziplocs of exposed film fill the camera bag to overflowing. Nina loses track of time. All she can think about is dancing with Angst, as she checks and rechecks which rolls he wants the lab to snip and what to hold back for later. The shooting and then the thank-yous go on and on. When they're finally packing his gear in the trunk of the rental, it's as though they've spent not merely the day but an entire season in Connecticut.

Angst puts the key into the ignition but doesn't start the car. Nina watches a small brown rabbit hop into the last rays of sunlight slanting across the lawn. Her focus zooms like a macro lens: the translucent flesh of its antenna-like ears, the wild blank eyes, the frantic beat of its tiny heart as it scans the sky for predators. She turns back to Angst, his chest slowly rising and falling as he stares through the windshield, his hands resting lightly on the steering wheel.

"So," he says, without looking at her. "Did you have fun?"

"Well, fun—I don't know about *fun*—"

There's no signal, no moment when it begins, it's simply happening—their hands everywhere, her skull hitting the dashboard as his weight bears down on her, then she's shimmying up to hang her head back through the open window as he pulls down her pants. Nina's coming as she sees the mother of the bride step through the front door of the house and then pause uncertainly.

"Angst—stop." Nina struggles to sit up, his fingers digging into the flesh of her arms as he pushes her back down. "*Rob.* Look up. Look *up.* Your client—at twelve o'clock."

"Aw, shit," he says, zipping up as she reins herself back into the bucket seat. "Do you think she saw you?"

"Did she see my head hanging out the window as you fucked me? Yeah—I'm thinking she did."

"All right, shut up, shut up. You just stay here. And pull up your pants."

Dust spews from the gravel of the homeowner's driveway as Angst turns the car around; they roll up their windows, adjust the vents to the AC. Red splotches ring Nina's upper arms where finger-shaped bruises are already rising to the surface.

"So?" she says, unable to wait any longer for him to speak.

"So, what?"

"So what did she *say?*"

"Nothing. Don't worry about it," he says, his eyes fixed on the road. "She asked for some extra cards."

"Well, then, maybe she didn't see anything—"

"Don't be stupid. This is Connecticut—she was just being polite."

"You're blaming me?"

"Did I say that? Look, Nina, I don't know—you said it yourself—we work together all the time. I'm just thinking that maybe for once I should do the right thing."

Nina says nothing as she takes this in. And then quietly, as though speaking to herself, she says, "Bing, bing, bing."

"*What?*"

"It's just something a friend of mine used to say—*bing, bing, bing, do the right thing.*"

Angst glances at her. "I don't get it," he says, his voice softening slightly. "Is it supposed to be funny?"

"Yes—no—never mind. I don't know why I said it."

They drive on in silence. Nina watches the numbers on the speedometer rise in the dimming light as Angst takes the shallow incline of the on-ramp to the interstate. *Whatever, whatever,* she says to herself. *Que sera, sera, what's done is done, day is done, gone the sun . . .* Her mind is a sputtering mess, her skin still on fire with longing, as she imagines each new set of oncoming headlights belongs to the car that will jump the median and smash into them. When they pull up safely in front of her building an hour later, Nina still pictures her bloodied body—all the particles of her being, all she's ever wanted—strewn across the highway.

"Thanks for your help today," Angst says, giving her a quick, light kiss and then one of his cards. "Send your invoice to my PO box. I've got to figure out where I'm going to live. Once I'm settled, I'll give you a call."

"Oh, that's right." She sticks the card into her back pocket. "Well, good luck with finding a place. And I am sorry about the fire, you know."

"I know. Pretty fucking crazy. But I guess that's life."

"All right, then," she says, opening the car door. "I'll see you. Good night."

"Good night, yeah, I'll see you soon. You take care now, okay?"

His voice echoes in her head as she wends her way up to her apartment. Nina laughs out loud in the vacant stairwell. *Take care?* A little late for that.

* *

The psychopharmacologist is a small sympathetic man with one brown eye and one blue who seems genuinely sorry when he tells her most people find coming off Nardil to be fairly unpleasant. In the days it takes for the lithium to build up in her bloodstream, Nina hears nothing from Angst. She spends them working with an unfamiliar crew on a dismal tabletop shoot for Macy's, her focus consumed with covering the distress generated by her withdrawal. A leaden exhaustion combined with a brittle agitation and an unnerving sense of déjà vu. As though each conversation, each four-piece place setting she wipes down with Windex is an experience foretold in a vivid dream that makes the reality painfully dim. The voice in her head is no longer Zen but boldly full of scorn and searing accusations of her ill-fated stupidity and incompetence. All day long she hopes to keep herself together, reaching desperation on the subway ride home—she's too shaky now to ride her bike. An ache swells inside her. At home, her body splayed on the living room floor, Nina weeps for no specific reason. Beyond the crest of the day, sadness floods through her in a drowning rush. Her arms outstretched, her wings melted, she plummets to the sea.

LAPSES | 1990

Despite the bitter wind tearing up the block, DJ found it peaceful on the limestone stoop. His hand trembled slightly as he lit a cigarette, but that was nothing new. *I don't want to die*, he thought, exhaling smoke up toward the budding maples that lined the street. Everything below him appeared garish in the sodium light, but above, in the clear black sky, a single star joined the waning moon, making a lyric-worthy image. He wished he wrote more songs instead of just noodling around. If he died now, what would his life have been?

Belinda was furious he'd started smoking again. If she knew he'd stopped taking the antiseizure meds ages ago, she would probably—what, kill him? Divorce him? What could she do except be madder and more disappointed. The Dilantin had only been a safety measure, prescribed in the first months after his stroke. And the last time his prescription expired, he hadn't seen the point of going back to the expensive neurologist, who could barely be bothered to crack open his chart. He'd been fine for years. The aneurysm that once defined his life and their relationship was ancient history. Or at least it had been. DJ felt her anger was misplaced, anyway. It was the memory lapses that had started him smoking—not the other way around. And he could think of worse things than a few hours lost in a pinball arcade. What difference did it really make if he couldn't remember how or when he got there?

Now he didn't want to go back inside, where Belinda and Nina were no doubt discussing him. DJ had slept with Nina once. A memory he kept tucked carefully away from what he otherwise derided as the "hopeful youth" of his pre-aneurysm days. When all his friends thought he would become a music journalist, the next Greil Marcus. Not a thirty-four-year-old clerk, barely making above minimum wage, in one of the handful of record stores left in Manhattan. He'd been dating Belinda then, more off than on. Had he already been having headaches then? He couldn't remember. He'd wanted to break things off with Belinda—he remembered that. But Nina had been living with a boyfriend she refused to leave, and their chance had passed. Now here she was single, and a good friend to them both, and he felt vaguely ashamed. She'd come over for dinner, not to referee. Maybe he could simply stay out here on the steps, forever.

"Just me," Nina said, when she came outside to retrieve him.

"And Belinda?"

"Oh, yeah," she said. "Still mad."

A dented gypsy cab slowed before them in the street. When the driver saw they weren't going anywhere, he stepped on the gas, tires squealing.

"*Nice*," Nina said, and then to DJ, "Guess both our brains have been fried." She sat down on the step above him and tapped her fist lightly on the side of his head. "But I suppose you trump me with that metal plate. Anybody in there?"

DJ knew she'd been in the hospital a few weeks herself, not that long ago, on a different sort of ward. Her manic reaction to antidepressants had been followed by months of deeper depression and destabilized mood, a condition she felt had only been made worse by that voluntary stay. It was a bad idea, she'd told him once, to leave the world completely. He wrapped his hand around her ankle.

"Bet you're glad you dragged yourself all the way out to Brooklyn."

"Yup. Been a regular laugh riot. My best visit *ever.*"

DJ blew smoke in a staccato of laughing breaths.

"So, you're having blackouts," Nina said.

"A couple," he said. "Actually, three."

"And that's why you're smoking. Because you're afraid."

"*Thank you*—yes, terrified."

"But you won't go to the doctor, and Belinda can't take you."

He'd thought she understood. Now he wasn't sure.

"You make it sound stupid," DJ said. "But Belinda gets migraines—"

"And she'll lose her job if she misses any more work, and you'll have no insurance and blah, blah, blah—yeah, I heard that too. And I have to tell you—right now? I'm not feeling all that sympathetic."

"Nina," he said. "C'mon. Don't."

"No, Deej—don't Nina me. She's your wife. And I know. She took care of you before. But she can't crumble *now*—whatever problems she's got. I care about Belinda, I do, but if I have to pick sides, then I'm choosing you, because I love you. And I don't want you to die—if it's all the same to your pigheaded self."

When he'd been in the hospital, the only time Nina came to visit he'd been out cold. But she'd left behind a vintage Superman comic, like some kind of talisman. DJ flicked his cigarette butt into the street.

"I know," he said, shaking her ankle. "It's okay. I love you too."

Nina pulled away. "*No*," she said. "Not like that. I'm saying I love you—big *L*—the other way."

He twisted his head around to see her face, half cast in shadow by her dark wavy hair. The anguish he saw filled him with a shameful gratitude and desperation.

"I may have noticed that," he said.

"So, what are you telling me now—that I'm transparent?"

"To me you are, yeah. Pretty much." The women he loved were always angry with him. "I feel the same, you know," he said. "I always have."

Nina bent forward, elbows to knees, and pressed her forehead into the heels of her hands. She was crying, but he was afraid to touch her. Then she slid down next to him and started to laugh.

"What," he said. "Tell me. What's funny?"

"It's just so melodramatic," she said, wiping away tears. "We're like daytime TV."

DJ hummed a plinking intro, then dropped the register of his voice. "*Like sands through the hourglass, so are the days of—*"

"Okay—*stop*. Just stop—you're killing me here. Let me tell you what we're going to do. We're going to go back inside and never mention this conversation—not to each other or to anyone else. I'm going to stay over and sleep on that uncomfortable old futon, and tomorrow Belinda can go in to work, and I'll take you to the doctor. End of story. Think you can do that?"

DJ nodded. Every door that ever opened with Nina was always quickly shut.

The next morning, along with mugs of coffee and slices of toast, tight smiles and embarrassed glances were passed around. No one pretended it hadn't been a rough night, but there was a tacit agreement among them to put the previous evening's upset behind as they all struggled to regain their equilibrium. The women went about their business—Belinda dressing for work, Nina phoning the doctor—and DJ retreated to his record collection.

Metal shelves sagging under hundreds of albums lined one entire wall of their living room from floor to ceiling. More stacks rose precariously from the floor, encroaching on the room. Beatles and bootleg Dylan; a rarely heard aria by Debussy; Elvis Presley to Elvis

Costello and all the one-hit wonders in between, collectors' editions shuffled among new and used vinyl of every genre.

He put on the Monkees' "Daydream Believer," a favorite of Belinda's. His use of the space and the money spent were sore points with her, even though music had originally joined them; he still loved to accompany her mournful country voice with a guitar. How could he stop buying records? Solely for its color and shape, he'd once given Nina a red heart-shaped single of Bobby Caldwell's "What You Won't Do for Love." Now it was an ironic symbol of his failure to act. DJ wondered if she still had it.

When it was time for Belinda to leave, the three of them stood awkwardly by the front door as she kissed him, her hand lingering on DJ's stubbled cheek.

"You look like hell," she said, and smiled.

"Ah," he said. "And I love you too."

"Don't let him smoke too much," she said, hugging Nina. "And thank you. I'm sorry—"

"No, no," Nina said. "I've got this—no need to be sorry." She left them there and went to try to get through to her doctor's office again.

Alone with his wife, DJ didn't know what to say.

"Who knows," Belinda said, kissing him again. "Maybe it'll turn out to be nothing."

"Maybe," he said. But he meant, *Don't go.*

After Belinda left, Nina joined him in the living room, where he'd been flipping through an old songbook. He laid the vintage Gibson back in its velvet-lined case.

"Okay, then," she said. "We're all set: three o'clock at East Sixty-Eighth—all the way by the river—so we'll need to leave time."

"I don't think I can do it," DJ said.

"Don't be silly, I'll be right there with you."

He could see she was on a mission. Her face was animated with a smile he found himself missing, even though she was sitting with a fresh cup of coffee on the couch beside him.

"Or in the waiting room, anyway. Or the hall," she said. "If you get a CT or whatever—since I'm not . . . I mean, I seriously doubt they'll let me come in, but maybe if we—"

"It's not that," he said. "It's not the doctor."

"Okay," she said. "Then what?"

"Last night—I don't think I can do that. Never say. Never do anything. When all I'm thinking is how much I want—" His voice thickened and caught in his throat as he tried not to cry. They were a hopeless pair. His living room was a terrible and shabby mess, his losses monumental. "I can't see—I mean . . . *why?* Why shouldn't I kiss you?"

DJ felt dizzy with emotion. He'd squeaked by death once already. What were the chances for a man with a hunk of metal stuck inside his head? Sitting not on his deathbed but a death-fold-out-futon. Begging a woman who was not his wife to let him kiss her. He loved Belinda, but he'd never been clearer about his feelings for Nina: she'd been—she was the one, if there was such a thing. Even as she held her hand up to his chest to stop him, he felt its warmth through the fabric of his T-shirt.

"You're just afraid," Nina said. Her voice was gentle. She scanned his face. "You don't really mean it," she said. "I'm afraid. *Belinda's* afraid. You can't—I shouldn't have said those things."

"Don't," he said. "Don't take it back. I'm glad you told me."

He let the tears run down his face. There was only one thing left for him to do. He put his hand on top of hers, and then he kissed her.

* *

Nina had wrangled a referral to another neurologist, and even though the doctor said she was welcome to join them, DJ asked her to wait outside; he didn't want to be distracted. When he told her he could barely think, she'd laughed and said, "Well, then, it's a good thing you're seeing a neurologist!" Whatever was wrong with his brain, he could still smell her skin.

The doctor studied the faxed pages of his chart.

"It's always good to get a second opinion," he said, and smiled.

DJ exhaled, momentarily relieved. He'd worried there'd be repercussions for his seeing someone else. "Thanks for fitting me in."

"I understand your friend out there is a force to be reckoned with. I hear she was quite . . . well, let's say *adamant* with my staff."

"What? *Oh—*" DJ started to stand.

"No, no—not a problem," the doctor said lightly. "Always good to have someone in your corner. Her physician's an old friend. I was just thinking you might like to tell her that she can relax. You have insurance?"

DJ sank back into the chair. He hadn't even thought to ask how she'd gotten him in.

"Yes, my wife—I'm . . ."

"Covered on her policy? That's fine," he said, making a note. "I'd like to send you up for a CT scan. Can you do that today?"

DJ nodded.

"So. You've been having disruptions. A sudden absence of memory—periods of lost time—is that correct?"

"That's right."

"And how many have you had?"

"Three."

"That's not so many," the doctor said, making another note. "And what do you do?"

"What do I *do*?"

"For work—yes—what do you do? Any heavy labor? That sort of thing."

"Just the occasional carton—I work in a record store."

The doctor smiled without looking up. "That's a sentimental vocation. And you're still taking Dilantan?"

"Actually, no—not for, well, not for a while—I can't remember exactly. Is that bad?"

"Not necessarily."

"Do you think . . . " DJ couldn't ask the question.

"That you'll have another aneurysm? I doubt it, but we'll do some blood work, and I'll look at a scan, and then we'll know if there's a serious problem. I'd like to put you on another antiseizure med, just to be on the safe side, and then we'll watch you for a while. How does that sound?"

"Good," DJ said. "That sounds good." He was happy to latch onto the doctor's optimism, to grab hold of anything that would tether him to life. Maybe a life with Nina—he could wait, he could see. "And the lapses? Do you—what do you—"

"What do I make of them? Not too much. These things can happen, even a long time after a severe event. It's like the brain taking a wrong neural turn in a familiar neighborhood where the road's never been repaired. It circles around for a while before finding its way back. Or the smallest skip in a record—you'd know about that—most times the needle scans past it. And then one day it sticks. Vinyl is soft; if the scratch is deep enough, the needle jumps, and because that track's ruined, some people might consider the record completely damaged, but that's not necessarily the case in my field. The brain has a tremendous capacity to heal itself. It learns to reroute."

* *

When his scans had come back normal, DJ felt heroic in his reprieve and found it easy to use his elation at being all right to cover the happiness generated by his liaison with Nina. Since their trip to the neurologist, he'd spent as much time with her as he could get away with. A month ago, he thought he might die; now here he was in the Greek diner around the corner from her place. The balding man behind the counter tipped his head in recognition.

"Rice pudding for you, my friend?"

"You got it," DJ said, pleased to have established himself as a regular customer.

He and Nina were like lovesick teenagers, unable to get enough. She was pale and uncharacteristically thin, always hankering for something sweet. He brought her rice pudding, iced black-and-white cookies, and Le Petit Écolier, packaged butter biscuits with a thick layer of milk chocolate embossed with an image of "the little schoolboy" bearing a basket of gifts—just as *he* was! The first time they met at her apartment, she'd been stunned when he confessed that, despite their comfortable physical affection, he and Belinda hadn't had sex these past few years.

"But that makes it so much more unfair!" she'd said. "Then it's not even about me—"

"Of course it is," he told her over and over. "And what's fair? It's too late for fair."

They'd gone back and forth, but there'd been no debating the chemistry between them.

He would always be grateful to Belinda. He couldn't have survived those first years after the aneurysm without her—and of course he'd loved and even married her. But given this second chance, he had to live his life. Love wasn't just dependency and paying the bills. In the canvas bag slung across his shoulder, DJ had the Decca rerelease of the dazzling 1959 recording of Stravinsky's *Firebird*, on CD because Nina didn't have a record player anymore. The lively wind instruments, oboe, flute, bassoon—the heartbreaking French horn solo at the end—even the harp and violins rendered from their sappy potential to something beautiful. That's what love was meant to be. Brilliant, like the firebird, a phoenix rising from the ashes into something new—he would tell her that—Nina, not Belinda. He didn't know what he would tell Belinda. She had to know on some level, didn't she? Their life had been good, but was the life that you fell into really good enough? He hadn't realized, hadn't thought about what it might mean to expect something more, but pressing the buzzer to Nina's apartment, he felt ablaze with love and all its promise.

Instead of hello, when she opened the door, Nina said, "She knows."

DJ tried to kiss her, but she moved away.

"Belinda? No—Nina, love—how could she know?"

"How could she know? I'll tell you how she could know. Because she keeps calling me, DJ, wanting to know why I'm avoiding her, why I don't return her calls. And I didn't—I couldn't—"

"You *told* her?" He let his bags slip to the floor.

"No, I didn't *tell* her—I'm not the one married to her, you know? She kept asking when we could get together, and I said, 'I'm sorry'—"

"You told her you were sorry," he said.

"I said I'm sorry, and she said . . ." Nina stopped and looked away; DJ wanted to shake her.

"What? What did she say?"

"She said, 'How could I have been so stupid?' And then she hung up."

For a moment they were silent, polarized. A thud of bass notes reverberated from an open car window two stories below, their rhythm at once familiar and utterly strange. DJ reached for her hand, the way suddenly clear.

"Marry me," he said.

"Not funny," Nina said, her hand slack in his. "Like that would make this all okay."

"I'm not joking—look, I brought you this." He pulled the CD from his bag. Nina ran her finger along its cellophane-wrapped edge.

"If I promise to marry you, you'll leave your wife."

"That would be the idea," he said, pulling her hand to his heart.

"Like a phoenix from the ashes. You think your marriage is ashes?"

"No," he said. "Yes—maybe, in a way—it's more like I was dead until I saw the flash of your brilliant feathers."

"Yeah, you mean my tail."

"I'm serious, Nina. Marry me."

"I don't know how it goes in the ballet," Nina said. "But in the myth, the hero's only charmed at the beginning. At the end, he comes to blame the firebird for all his troubles."

Outside in the street, there was still the thumping of music. Nina walked to the window and looked down. Beside her, its neck resting on the arm of a small upholstered chair, was the old acoustic he'd given her, a good beginner's guitar with a decent sound. A chart of chords lay on the floor. He'd been teaching her to play.

"What's that asshole doing?" she said loudly, her back to DJ. And then more quietly, without turning around, "We're not albums you can just exchange, one for the other. You'd have to leave her—leave Belinda first, and *then*—then we could see. I can't marry you based on sex and rice pudding. And I couldn't—I wouldn't take care of you the way she does; you'd have to be your own person. I can barely support myself."

Her rebuke didn't dim his hopes—he crossed the room to where she stood, wrapped his arms around her from behind—he'd heard her phrasing, *you'd have to.* She was considering it; he had only to wait for the reprise. They heard a double honk, and then the shuddering bass line receded as they watched the black four-by-four slowly roll down the block and turn up Second Avenue.

"With you," he said, softly, "I could do that—I could do anything."

DJ touched the wrought-iron rail of the stoop for luck, and then, wary of their slippery and chipped linoleum—all he needed now was to fall and crack his skull—he climbed the sagging interior steps leading up to their apartment. When he came through the door, it was so still and quiet that he wondered if he could have somehow gotten home before her. He'd pictured broken records, or Belinda fiercely slamming pots and pans—though she would hardly be cooking dinner for her unfaithful husband. Still, he found the silence more alarming than any imagined attack, any litany of rightful accusations. The whole subway ride home he'd been bracing himself, certain of her impending fury. On the kitchen counter, amid dirty dishes and breakfast crumbs, sat a bag of groceries. Chicken cutlets and broccoli; Orangina and a bottle of Absolut, the makings of a cocktail they'd often enjoyed; two pints of Häagen-Dazs, coffee and raspberry vanilla swirl, their respective favorites, halfway melted. He couldn't sort out the timeline. Had she bought them before or after calling Nina? Brought them home and left? Where would she go?

"Linney?" he called out, walking down the junk-filled hall, his pulse quickening as he wove through the back room overflowing with books and Belinda's sketches, Gocco silk screens, jewelry, and her other half-finished craft projects; keyboards and mic stands;

rolled and ruined rock posters, probably worth something if they'd been preserved. He tripped on a rack of hand-washables and stumbled through the doorway into their bedroom.

"In here," he heard her say, but her voice was so small he couldn't be sure if she'd said "in" or "I'm."

Belinda lay fully clothed on their unmade bed, still in the forties-style wool coat that was the pride of her thrift-store finds, and a colorful scarf, one stockinged foot bare, the other still in a narrow-heeled pump. She worked as a legal secretary at a small boutique firm that handled Soho galleries and artists, which allowed for her quirky fashion style and, encouraging the artistic endeavors of all their employees, even paid for her drawing classes. Her arm was flung across her face, leaving only her mouth, still freshly lipsticked, in view. She had classic full lips; in mocking dark shades and vintage hats she often jokingly posed, capturing the glamour of old-fashioned movie stars. If he hadn't heard her speak, he might not have been sure that she was breathing. Belinda. His wife. His girl.

When he knelt at the edge of the bed, she rolled over on her side, turning away.

"I could see how—I know we don't—"

"Belinda." He put his hand on her shoulder. She didn't push it away.

"And I know there's history. But *Nina*." She turned back to him now, her pale blue eyes wide open, unfocused with pain. "How could she betray me that way?"

DJ let a week go by, and then another, before he called Nina from the record store. He still hadn't told Belinda that he was leaving.

"I just need a little time," he said.

Nina laughed, a harsh singular sound. "'Time Is on My Side'—the Rolling Stones; 'Time Has Come Today'—the Chambers Brothers; 'Give Me Just a Little More Time'—Chairmen of the Board—remember that one? Should I go on? Oh, wait—'Time in a Bottle'—by what's-his-face. No, no, don't tell me—big fat mustache . . . *Jim Croce.* I rock. I *roll.* Don't you think I roll?"

"Nina, c'mon—"

"Nina, c'mon? Ding, ding, ding—that does sound familiar, but it doesn't fit the category. You mean 'Come On *Eileen.*' I'm the one who's stupid."

"*No,*" he said. You're *not.* I'm—"

"Sorry? Wrong again. I'm not Uncle Albert."

"But I am sorry. And I should have called. I should have called sooner. I'm leaving work early today, and I can come by on my way—"

"Home?"

She was right. He'd tell Belinda this evening. Stalling was pointless—wouldn't make things any easier—he was losing Nina and he couldn't let her go.

"'Better Be Home Soon,'" DJ said. "Crowded House. I'll see you later, okay?"

On the platform at Sixty-Third and Lex, the sounds of a vibraphone filled the hot stale air. A white kid in a hooded sweatshirt and white leather high-tops was playing a version of "My Funny Valentine" to rival Chet Baker's. DJ pulled a dollar from his pocket, and his crumpled grocery list fell to the ground and was swept onto the tracks by the rush of commuters heading toward the Brooklyn-bound F. DJ set his dollar among the coins and bills in the busker's upturned hat and boarded the train. He imagined Nina, in her apartment, waiting for him to arrive. He'd intended to buy her Melitta filters, 2-percent milk, and rice pudding. By the time the train rose aboveground on the Brooklyn side, she'd have figured out he wasn't coming.

He climbed up the subway steps at Prospect Park, feeling relieved that he was doing the right thing. But when he got to his building, he couldn't bring himself to go in. He sat on the stoop to smoke a last cigarette, and an hour later he was still sitting there when Belinda came home.

"Are you coming or going? Unbelievable," she said, brushing past him.

"No—wait." He reached up and held her sleeve. "I'm here."

Belinda resisted but then said, "All right." She glanced at the crumpled pack of Winstons at DJ's feet. "Come inside," she said. "It's freezing out here—you'll make yourself sick."

As DJ was hanging up his coat, he heard breaking glass, and he found Belinda in the kitchen holding shards of a vintage tumbler she loved.

"It's nothing," she said, and dropped the pieces into the trash. "Why don't you put on a record?"

For once he couldn't imagine what he wanted to play.

PHOTO FINISH | 1999

1. Mick

After the divorce and two rounds of rehab, he didn't see his daughter often. Miraculously, Stacey hadn't poisoned her against him, but he maintained a distance that would keep Jesse's expectations low. Mick's sobriety remained a tentative thing, so he steered away from birthdays and holidays, with a vaguely seasonal regularity in mind. It had taken him a long time to pick up a camera again, to quiet the past and his own expectations of himself enough to let the day lead him where it would in service of a series of photos that captured a particular experience: that sharp moment of instantaneous connection with a stranger. Most people on the street shied away from his camera, but there were always those who would boldly look into the lens. And the best, the shots he loved most, were of women who'd passed by but looked back, or even spun around for a step, to see if they'd been in the frame. There was a seasonal quality to these pictures, too, taken from the shelter of entrances—to Grand Central, Penn Station, and busy Midtown office buildings—or at cafés with outdoor seating, where he could linger over coffee and make notes about the day. A fantasy, really, that it would add up to a show, but it kept him engaged in the moment.

He worked part-time now, in the photography department at B&H, supplementing his income with corporate portraits. Gigs that were both steady and staid. Some days, he was still haunted by the wish for glamour and fame that once drove a career he'd done his best to sabotage. But mostly, he just wanted to make something *good.* Though he still hoped—he still needed—for the work to find a place in the world. A pending snowstorm had cut short his winter's visit with Jesse, but today, with the buds just beginning to show on the trees, he meant to gift her his old Pentax ME.

2. Jesse

"Just *go,*" she said, "I'll be fine."

"Oh, sure," said Stacey. "I'm just gonna leave my thirteen-year-old daughter standing around by herself, in the lobby of the Plaza Hotel. Maybe next time he can have you meet him in Times Square. Or the Port Authority Bus Terminal—that'd be a good place. What's the plan, anyway? Tea and crumpets at The Palm Court? A horse and carriage ride?"

"Hardly. And those horses are *sad*—I'd never do that. We're just gonna go for a walk in the park."

"In the park? It's fucking freezing."

"*Mom.*"

"It's freakin' freezing. Okay?"

"I've got gloves."

"She's got gloves," Stacey said to a passing bellhop. "It's forty degrees out, but she's got gloves."

"Did you need help with something?" the bellhop said.

"Where do I start?"

"We're *fine,*" said Jesse. "Thank you."

The bellhop tipped his hat, continued rolling his car toward the entrance.

"*Tuh,*" Stacey said. "Did you see that? Who tips their hat anymore?"

Jesse studied the entrance, losing a bet with herself on which one of the three revolving doors her dad would come through.

"There he is."

"Oh, thank fucking God. Because this poshness is suffocating."

"Do you always have to be so—"

"So what? What am I so?"

Jesse took a deep breath. Each time she met up with her dad, her mom lost her shit. "So Whac-A-Mole," she said, the words a barely audible confession. Once, when she was little, according to family lore, Jesse had gone nuts with the plastic mallet, banging around the whole apartment, making for a running joke between her parents, an inside expression for getting carried away.

"Oh, my girl." Stacey pulled her into a hug. "I just don't want you to get hurt."

"I'm not. I won't," Jesse said, but she usually did. Her dad was . . . She didn't know what he was. Sometimes he seemed so beaten down—like those carriage horses. Or like she was the carriage horse. Each of them holding out a stub of carrot, maybe a sugar cube. And he *had* taken her on a carriage ride one time. She must've been seven, maybe eight, when it still seemed a thrilling thing to do. When she couldn't see how worn the head feathers were in the horse's bridle. When she'd noted but not understood the carriage man's leer.

3. Mick

The day was colder than he would've liked for their walk, but it warmed if he kept to the sunnier paths in Central Park, a place that had drawn him since he was a kid of Jesse's age, and, keeping pace beside him, she didn't seem to mind. She would not expect, when they stopped for lunch, that the camera around his neck was for her.

"Uncle Elliot sent me a lobster claw."

"What?"

"Your brother," she said.

"Yeah, I got that part."

Jesse smiled at her own little joke. "For my birthday." She formed her gloved fingers into the shape of a box, looked up to see if she had his full attention. "One of those shiny white boxes, like for jewelry? With that really soft cotton inside. But instead of a necklace or whatever . . ." She shaped her hands like biting puppets now, snapping at the air. "A lobster claw, partly covered with gold leaf."

"So he's still stuck on that, then," Mick said, half to himself.

"What do you mean?"

"He was doing twigs and acorns, that kind of thing—antiquing them, I suppose, with gold or silver leaf. Something about the preciousness of nature. But he'd have had to boil and eat the lobster, so a little weird, no?"

"I don't know. It's kind of beautiful. *He's* kind of weird, though."

"You saw him?"

"No," said Jesse. "Just what I remember." She paused, her lips pursed to the side and one eye squinted—an expression he recognized as Stacey's. "Quietly seething."

He laughed. "*Seething*, yes—that's my brother all right. Where'd you get that word?"

"I read and I'm not stupid—I live in the world."

"Sorry," Mick said, helpless before her.

Jesse kicked a pebble from the path. "It's all right."

"Don't be mad. What can I do?"

"Don't do *that*—get all beg-y."

Mick tried not to laugh. "Okay, okay. Mea culpa." He could give her the camera now, but it would seem like a bribe. He should call Elliot, see if *he's* all right. Lobster claws. They were coming up on Strawberry Fields, and he'd been thinking of Sarabeth's Kitchen. "Should we keep walking, or get some food?"

"Walk," she said. Then, after a moment, "What's mea culpa?"

"Latin," said Mick, "for my fault."

4. Jesse

"So?" her mom said the second Jesse came through the door. "How was it?"

"Is that what you're calling him now?" Jesse thought her comeback clever; her mom, who was putting away the vacuum, did not. "Just a joke."

"I know. I got it. Ha ha ha. It's your life. You wanna keep it some big secret, that's fine with me."

Jesse glanced around. They kept up the kitchen, but she couldn't remember the last time her mom had vacuumed. It didn't seem a good sign. "We had lunch at Sarabeth's."

"Ah, the popovers."

"I had a waffle, but yeah."

"Looks good in here, doesn't it?"

Her mom hadn't so much cleaned as straightened up the piles, though she'd cracked open one of the windows facing the street to let in the fresh air. "Spring cleaning?"

"Not really. It just seemed like time. So waffles and then he bought you a camera—with his discount, I suppose."

"It's his old Pentax—he says he's not using it anymore."

"Oh, well—in that case. Does he plan on paying for film and processing?"

Jesse lifted the strap from around her neck. "I don't know. I guess. Who says I'm gonna use it?"

Her mom bent her head forward, pressed her hands to her eyes, her elbows extended like some peculiar sculpture, then let out a small groan. "Don't let me fuck this up," she said. "You want to take pictures, you should. I can think of worse things."

5. *Mick*

A week later, in the Donut Pub on the corner of Fourteenth Street and Seventh Avenue, Mick drank a black coffee and savored a honey-glazed, down to sucking the last bits of sugar from the tip of his index finger and his thumb. If he called, Elliot wouldn't answer—if he was even there. The trip worth it for the donut, either way.

Just a few doors west, Elliot's wedge of a studio apartment sat halfway below the street but included a wide shallow-set window at sidewalk level, its interior sill serving as a miniature gallery. Even as kids, Elliot had collected bits of found things. A stray jack, a gumball ring, a flip top from a beer can that featured, Mick had to admit, a particularly graceful curl. Wrought-iron bars offered meager protection for the window, and there was a yellowed shade Elliot could pull down at night, though the light from the street would've had to leak in around it, a slivered view of people's shoes forever moving back and forth. You could actually open that window, but Mick couldn't imagine the noise and the filth—Elliot's place, however cheap the rent might be, essentially in the gutter.

People veered around him as Mick bent toward the glass, cupping his hands to view the objects displayed. A lobster claw like the one Jesse had described, a short branch of red coral spottily covered with gold leaf in a way that made you think of dappled light, and a pair of oak leaves whose veins and edges were also tipped in gold. The textures and fragility startled, despite the dirty glass. Crouching farther down, he could see his half brother's legs from the knee down, a clog dangling from a ragg-socked and jiggling foot. Elliot no doubt reading or listening to music in an armchair he'd found on the street and reupholstered in a bottle-green velvet, his studio a triangular cave filled with jewel-toned objects.

Awash in the huff of exhaust from a crosstown bus, Mick tapped on the glass. His head bent to his side of the window, Elliot's expression seemed to expand and contract in a kaleidoscope of emotions, from fury to surprise, then annoyance to an eye-rolling giving in. *So dramatic*, Mick thought as he waited to be buzzed in. It didn't miss his notice that he'd married someone equally as histrionic.

"You don't call, you don't write," Mick said, raising his voice over the bittersweet chorus of Crowded House. *Hey now, hey now.* "Do you never get tired of that song?"

"You came here to bash my taste in music?"

"No one's bashing anything. I can't drop in on my own half flesh and blood in his half an apartment?"

"Well, you're here now." Elliot lowered the sound on his archaic boom box. "No donut for me?" He raised his chin and Mick looked down at his peacoat, brushed away flakes of glaze.

"Coals to Newcastle, I thought."

Elliot offered him coffee.

"Nah, I'm good." Mick sat down on the end of Elliot's single bed, half of it covered in decorative pillows.

"So how are you, Ellie?"

"Holding up," he said, busying himself with an electric kettle and a single-cup Melitta. "How 'bout you? How's the straight and narrow?"

"One donut at a time. I hear you sent Jesse a lobster claw."

Elliot turned around, a spoon skittering off the cutting board set on top of the half fridge and clanking into the tiny metal sink. "Did she not like it? What'd she say?"

"*Kinda beautiful*, I believe, were her exact words."

"Oh, good—that's good. I mean, I thought she'd get it, but I couldn't be sure."

Elliot's face opened in a sparkling pride that snagged at Mick's heart, the feeling hard to bear. "She said *you* were kind of weird."

"Ha—well, that's true."

"So you're really okay, then? Here in your little cave with your . . ." Mick turned to the window. "Your gilded crustaceans?"

"I could make you one, if that's what you're angling toward."

"Oh, *angling*—ha. I do like the coral. Where do you get it?"

Elliot stirred milk and honey into his coffee.

"Well, that's gross," said Mick.

"To each his own. There's a place on Delancey that sells aquariums and such."

"Like those little Diver Dans?"

"That show gave me the creeps. But yeah."

"You should gold leaf one of those little treasure chests."

Elliot sat down in the velvet chair. "Will you be staying for dinner?"

Mick laughed, genuinely this time. It was an old joke; neither of them cooked worth a damn. "Are we having lobster?"

"Don't be stupid. I get the claws from one of the cooks at the Chinese."

"You still go to that place over on Bethune? We could order in."

"Or you could just tell me whatever it is that's on your mind. Because the banter? It's wearing me down."

Mick's card was maxed out, Elliot's reserved for prop and furniture rental, fresh flowers, and other styling supplies. So they pooled what cash they had and ordered in, mostly off the appetizer menu with a token nod toward some broccoli with garlic sauce.

"You will receive an uninvited guest," Elliot read from the slip of the fortune cookie he'd cracked open before setting out the containers on two collapsible TV trays in front of the bed.

"Give me that." *You will meet a handsome stranger*, was what it actually said. Mick waved the paper like a little flag.

"Yes, *meet*," said Elliot. "But then what?"

"Ah, well, that's the hard part, isn't it. I dread the day when Jesse . . ."

"I'm sure." Elliot divvied up egg rolls and triangles of shrimp toast, tore open the steaming bag of ribs. "Was there something, though, Mick? That brought you crosstown? Not that this isn't delightful."

Mick couldn't say why it was that he'd come, beyond a pretense of worry—though he did worry about Elliot. Worried about him staying home in his little cave; worried about him getting beat up on Fourteenth Street.

"Why couldn't it be?"

"Delightful?"

Mick bit into an egg roll that was much too hot. He waved his hand before his mouth, and Elliot opened him a can of ginger ale.

Mick gulped the soda, nearly spit up from the fizz, then wiped his nose and mouth on the back of his hand.

"That was certainly delightful." Elliot handed him a stack of takeout napkins.

"Ginger ale?" said Mick. "Who drinks ginger ale?"

"Free soda with any order over fifteen bucks. You didn't specify."

"And you didn't say I needed to."

"*Mick.*"

"What?"

Elliot carefully wiped the glaze from the ribs off his fingers. "Just tell me you're not dying, okay?"

"Why would I be dying?"

As though the reason should be obvious, Elliot's gaze dipped down to Mick's elbow and back.

"I was never shooting up. Jesus, Elliot. You're the one . . ."

"That is true." Elliot rolled up the fortune and slid it into the open keyhole of the soda can. "But one would have to . . . you know. Little chance of that."

"Sorry," Mick said, the word a catchall for everything he had and hadn't done.

"So you're not dying."

"Not that I know of."

"What *are* you doing here, then?"

"I have to be dying to stop by?"

Elliot put his hands to his face and shook his head.

"Okay, okay," said Mick. "I really don't know." He wiped the eggroll through a pool of duck sauce, then set it back down on the paper plate. "My life feels . . . strange. Dislocated, somehow. I just wanted to see you."

"Fine, then. Here I am. Just don't touch my duvet with those greasy fingers."

The subway uptown was still crowded, and Mick watched empty tracks and an unused platform covered in graffiti flicker past, his reflection returning to the door's glass panel in the narrow, one-way stretches of tunnel. *You're her dad*, Elliot had said, when he told him he'd given Jesse a camera, but Mick could see he was hurt. Had he meant to one-up him, to diminish Elliot's artistic gift? Their conversation couldn't wander very far, and Jesse was usually a safe zone. Unlike the world of commercial photography in which Elliot still worked, their clients overlapping at one time, Mick's often coke-based popularity had been a barbed thorn in his half brother's side. Elliot being known equally for the perfection of his work and the conflicts with photographers and art directors that it often caused.

Once, in frustration at a troublesome drape in the background of a packaging shot for some Battenberg pillow shams, he'd thrown a staple gun across the set, making a small triangular tear in the duvet, the client's only photo sample. *Battenberg.* Such a stupid detail to recall. But Elliot had gone on and on about it at the time, and the name of a German city known for its lace had stuck. If he hadn't been rushed, Elliot claimed, if his assistant had been worth a damn, if the client had a clue . . . everyone else to blame for him losing his temper. At least he showed up—the category in which Mick had most often faltered. *Failures for $1000, please.* Sleeping through a gig. Losing a crucial roll of film. Where Elliot cared too much, Mick had had trouble bothering; Stacey's voice in his ear, always telling him what a fuck-up he was. And though he'd done some good personal work, he hadn't done much to promote it. That was the truth of it right there—he hadn't really tried.

As though success would come to him because he deserved it. Looking back, he—like everyone else—found it hard to believe that he did.

The bigger question was what could he—what would he—do now? People fell into the shadows of rehab, their lives revolving around meetings and expectations set deliberately low; he'd certainly been carrying on that way. To raise the bar could so easily result in the thing landing square on your head. He imagined it, this metaphorical bar, not as the light pole of a gymnastic vaulter, but a heavy and rusted I-beam. Raise that fucker up at your own . . . what was the word? Risk, yes, but more than that. *Peril.* Because the danger was more than failure. Breakdown, even death.

When he was in photo school, out in Santa Barbara, he'd known a guy, a brilliant sculptor who'd coked himself up into a manic episode, falling just this side of a long tenure in the psych ward, thanks to family connections. Last he heard, the guy was making custom kitchen cabinets. Not unlike the corporate portraits Mick took to help cover the rent on his East Harlem apartment. He was still shooting, though; he still had ideas. Tomorrow, if the weather was good, he'd go down to Bethesda Fountain. Something about the layered history of that spot, from his own adolescence. Hours spent hanging there before concerts in the park. The kids perched on park benches that had populated his best shots, their raw and challenging energy. Maybe he'd negotiate with Stacey for another day with Jesse. The two of them together less of a stalker-y endeavor.

6. *Mick*

Courtesy of spring break, he and Jesse ambled through Strawberry Fields on an early Wednesday afternoon, her first time out with the

Pentax, which he'd helped her load with black-and-white film. The day was warm but overcast, the park mostly populated by nannies and their charges, the ubiquitous roller skaters and bicyclers racing past, and walkers of small, overly precious dogs. Jesse seemed equal parts interested in and skeptical of their endeavor.

"So you just wander around and ask people if you can take their picture?"

"Yes and no," he said. "I try to settle down somewhere, the way you might if you were watching birds or some untamed animal you wanted to observe. Relax enough so that people get curious—*watcha looking at?* That kind of thing."

"Like David Attenborough."

Mick laughed. "But without the accent. So Stacey still loves that shit, huh?"

"She does."

"But I also try to engage. See what people are up to, what they think."

"What they think?"

"People that are hanging or maybe hiding out, here in the park, or some spot on the street. What they think about life"—he opened his arm toward a stand of maples just beginning to leaf out—"of the world at large."

Jesse nodded toward the dog run beside the near-empty playground. "Central Park hardly seems the world at large."

"Well, the world around them, then. I just try to get them talking. It's like . . ."

She waited for him to go on, and Mick felt the pressure of his enterprise. Could he, should he really explain what he tried to shoot? His own sense of exclusion and isolation? And the strength of connection he often felt with strangers? People he'd never have to see again.

"Sometimes," he said, "when you meet someone in a passing moment—a moment that'll never repeat—they'll share something with you that they didn't even know they wanted or needed to say. And the silence that follows? That's when I snap the picture."

"You *see* them."

"Yes."

7. Nina

This was the good and the bad thing about living in Manhattan: you were bound, eventually, to bump into everyone you'd ever slept with. Although Nina's friends, most having abandoned the city years ago, claimed this was a knack all her own. Celebrity sightings—sure. The occasional blast from the past? Most people had that experience. But something different happened for Nina, a kind of prescience, a physical feeling. Sometimes she would just know, stepping out of a subway station, that she was going to run into someone. More rarely was this, what was happening to her right now. She was walking through Central Park, coming up on Bethesda Fountain, thinking of a concert she'd once ducked out of her Fresh Meadows high school to attend, tagging along with a girl she'd been trying to impress. New Riders of the Purple Sage—she hadn't even known who they were.

The girl, whose name she'd long forgotten, had an older boyfriend who drove a station wagon, and on their way into the city from Queens, they'd stopped off at the upstairs apartment of a run-down two-family house to pick up some of his friends. Wondering how much longer they'd be there, if they wouldn't miss the concert at this rate, Nina had noted the paucity of furniture, the stains and cigarette burns on the corduroy loveseat where the girl sat giggling on her boyfriend's lap, and then, stepping into what she'd thought would be the bathroom, Nina had come upon the guy they'd apparently been waiting for, who was shooting up.

In the park, the air was warm but she felt a chill, a kind of shiver of recognition as a man and what appeared to be his daughter—twelve? maybe thirteen? a camera slung around each of their necks—came strolling around the fountain. *I know you*, her body said, as the man met her gaze and quickly looked away, his hand lightly steering the girl toward the shadowed row of arches below the terrace. *Mick*. The name rose up in her mind. Along with the bit of debauchery that had cost her a job in the display department of Bloomingdale's. A job she'd hated, but still. Given the chance to do it over? Nina felt a wave of despair for her younger self, not so very different from the woman she was now. Knowing what she'd learned—not just about him, but the slim chances for happiness in life—would she have made the same choice? Taken the moment and let the rest be damned? There'd been a quality about him, a strange blend of attraction and repulsion, that had drawn her in.

Was this girl the baby who'd been screaming in the background when, at her boss's insistence, Nina called him at home to ask where the film was? Had his wife—who'd given her a scathing earful when she asked for Mick—stayed with him? Nina could still remember the plaid of the pearl-snapped shirt he'd been wearing the day they met in her boss's cramped office. As though it was the shirt and not a tiny origami envelope of coke that had fueled their foolish night together. She'd been a dabbler in the seamier side of things, curious but lacking whatever it was that took people all the way down.

His daughter, or whoever this girl was, looked back at her, and Nina resisted the urge to wave. It probably wasn't even him, just the spray from the fountain giving her a chill, the familiar bones of the place dredging up a maudlin mix of memories. The girl raised her camera, Nina heard the whirr of the shutter, and then she passed out.

8. Mick

"You have to do something," said Jesse, but he shook his head—there were plenty of other people around and, keeping his voice down, he said as much. The woman had looked familiar, though he couldn't say from where, and he didn't want the past to destroy what, so far, had been a lovely afternoon. But Jesse wouldn't let it go.

"She looked straight at me. I took her picture. And *then* she fell—like I'd literally shot her."

"It's just a photo—throw out the film if it bothers you. But you didn't *do* anything."

A few people had formed a loose circle around the woman, but no one stepped forward.

"You mean like you're doing now?"

Mick looked at his daughter, her face a poster for that fierce teenage sense of injustice.

"All right, all right. Hold this." Jesse took his camera, and Mick knelt down, put his hand to the woman's cheek, which was cool to his touch. He looked back up at the people nearby. "Don't just stand there gawking—someone go call an ambulance." At his voice, the woman stirred. *Shit*, thought Mick, *I know you.*

"What are you *doing*?" The woman pushed him away, frantically patted around for her bag, finding it slipped from her shoulder but still wrapped around her arm.

His hands raised in a show of innocence, Mick leaned away.

She tried to sit up but was clearly dizzy.

"She shouldn't move," someone called out.

"I got it," said Mick.

Jesse knelt down beside him. "Is she okay?"

"My head," the woman said. "What happened?"

"Don't know. I think you fainted." Mick shrugged off his jacket, tucked it under her head.

Of the people who'd stopped, only a woman with a shivering Yorkie remained. "You shouldn't move her," she said, the same voice as before.

"Are you a doctor?" said Jesse.

"No. But that's what they always say on TV."

"Well, this isn't TV, is it?" said Mick.

"C'mon, Trixie," the onlooker said. "They don't want our help, they don't have to have it."

"*Trixie?*" said Jesse. "You gotta be kidding."

"You took my picture," the woman said.

"I'm *so* sorry. Here," she said, clawing at the side of the Pentax, "I'll dump the film."

"You have to press the button on the bottom," said Mick.

"*No*," said the woman. "Don't. It's all right. I'm all right." She looked at Mick. "Can you help me sit up?"

"Someone went for an ambulance—at least I think they did. Could be a while, and you probably shouldn't move."

She put her hand to the back of her head, and two fingers came back with fresh blood. "Listen, Mick—I'm not gonna lie here all day waiting for some ambulance that is or isn't going to come."

"What did you say?"

"I'm not gonna—"

"No, my name—you said my name."

"You know her?" said Jesse.

"No," the woman said. "Yes. I'm not sure."

"What's your name?" said Jesse.

"Nina."

"*Nina*," said Mick. "From Bloomingdale's. What are the fucking odds."

9. *Nina*

On a snowy Saturday, when Nina was fifteen, she and a friend had taken hits of blotter acid. They'd started out in the children's section of the public library, where they'd flipped through the pages of *Madeleine*, *Babar*, and *Curious George* waiting for the high to come on. Kicked out for being too loud, they'd moved on to Gertz, a small now-defunct department store, where they'd spent the rest of the afternoon in the furniture department. Each room set like its own foreign territory as they wandered about for what felt like days; each object outlined in the same iridescence that trailed from their hands like a sparkler's glow. They sat themselves down on the end of beds, on nubby couches and leather recliners, marveling at the connectivity between all things and other grand revelations. The whole experience like a lovely land to which they'd never again return; their trip an Eden-like peg in determining a life of happiness glimpsed, then lost as easily as an ecstatic afternoon might fade into a dull and ordinary evening. Only passing out in Central Park and hours spent in a crowded ER with a recovered cokehead would reveal the startling association: Nina had spent years of her life in department stores and photo studios, arranging room sets and other displays.

"No sleeping before bedtime," the discharge nurse said, holding Nina's paperwork out to Mick.

"Oh—" he said, "no—we're not—"

"I'll take those," said Nina.

"Well, someone will have to wake her every couple of hours, ask her a simple question. What her name is, does she know where she is."

I'm standing right here, Nina wanted to say. She had a large bump on the back of her head and a small cut from a stray piece of glass that had required a few stitches. The doctor wanted to admit her overnight for observation, but Nina, insurance-less, had declined. The ER bill alone would absorb any advance she might get on her credit card. Somewhere between a blood pressure and a blood sugar drop, she'd passed out—nothing that a donut wouldn't fix. Better than the watery orange juice and cheap chocolate chip cookie she'd been given along with confirmation of what she already knew. She hadn't been eating because she'd been nauseated, and she'd been nauseated for the most inconvenient reason an unattached woman could have. Whether she had a concussion wasn't clear, but she was meant to take the necessary precautions. All she wanted to do was go to sleep, to forget about the decision she would have to make, not to mention Mick and his anxious daughter. She'd tried to get them to go home—Mick had obviously wanted to. But Jesse refused, saying he could do what he wanted, a line whose sharpness, bloody head aside, Nina couldn't miss. She didn't feel any more poorly than she had before she fell, and her elbow, having hit the ground first, hurt more than her head. She'd have to steer clear of Bethesda Fountain if she was always going to be running into them.

Nina stuffed the papers into her bag. "Not a problem." She would set an alarm and ask herself the goddamn questions. The unknowing father had taken a job on the West Coast—a move that, among other things, had driven them apart. And he was the last person she felt like calling, even if he weren't three thousand miles away. In the future, when you could beam across the country at will, you would be even harder-pressed to avoid your exes and one-night stands.

10. Mick

"So you have someone?" he said, out on the street. "Someone who'll come over?" Mick remembered Nina, not because of the night they'd spent, but because, as far as Stacey was concerned, it had marked the end of their marriage. The last straw, the straw that broke the camel's back—why was there always a straw? Nina looked like a straw, standing there by the curb, as if the slightest wind might blow her down. At least she'd already be at the hospital.

"Sure," Nina said.

"No, she doesn't," said Jesse.

"*Jesse*," Mick said.

"If she did, she'd have already called them, wouldn't she."

Mick had not been thrilled to have to call Stacey to say they'd be late because they'd been helping a woman who'd fallen in the park. *So you're a good Samaritan now*, she'd said. *Is that one of the steps?* There were not enough amends in the world for Stacey, but he'd certainly made up for anything he'd owed Nina today.

"I'll be fine," Nina said.

"Oh—I know," said Jesse. "You could call her, and then if she's *dead*, if she doesn't pick up, you could call 911."

He might've laughed if she weren't his daughter, if a cutting sarcasm beyond the native bounds of adolescence wasn't largely his fault. You couldn't live with a person like Stacey and not have her critical bent and its wounded self-righteousness infect your life. Plus,

Jesse had a point. A better person wouldn't shuffle Nina off in a cab, jettisoning her back into her own life, the one in which his part was ancient history. Had he said anything more about Nina than that they'd once worked together on a shoot, Jesse would've been more than glad to have their ruined afternoon and its absurd coincidences come to a close. What had compelled her to take Nina's photo? And why, in spite of it all, was he eager to see the shot? Nina held her arm high, the cabs whizzing past, and Mick resisted the urge to snap her picture himself. What kind of a man was he?

"Would you want me to do that?"

"Call me in the middle of the night?"

Her tone was facetious, her arm still in the air as she faced him. Mick placed a hand on Jesse's shoulder. "I'd have to get her home and take care of a few loose ends. But I could stay on your couch or whatever. Make sure you're all right." Her arm dropped. For a second he thought she might smack him, but then he could see that Jesse was right. *In for a dime, in for a pint of blood*, as Elliot would say. "If there's no one else."

Nina pressed her hands to her face as though hoping he and his daughter, maybe the entire world, would go away. Mick looked at Jesse. But she just nodded toward Nina—her eyes wide in emphasis, her mouth an insistent line—as if repeating her earlier exhortation that he do something to help. He glared back, mocking her expression. *She's not some stray puppy*, he wanted to say. Instead, he lightly touched Nina's arm. "You okay?"

Her hands slid down to her chin. "What a fucking day. Am I right?"

This time Mick did laugh—but he was the only one.

"No—it's funny," said Nina. "It is." She felt for the gauze taped to the back of her head. “Not the worst idea, I suppose. You coming over.”

She wrote her number and address on the back of a Rite Aid receipt. And that was how they began.

ACKNOWLEDGMENTS

This collection is true to my heart, and my deepest thanks go to those who have helped, in one way or another, along the way.

Brooke Warner, Shannon Green, Cait Levin, Julie Metz, Kiran Spees, and the rest of the team at She Writes Press. Caitlin Hamilton and Rick Summie. Tom Jenks, Olga Zilberbourg, Mimi Kusch, Jen Knox, Jen Michalsky, Will Allison, and Tam Putnam. Dominic Smith, Peter Turchi, Kevin McIlvoy, Joan Silber, Ronit Plank, Louise Marburg, Caitlin Horrocks, Daisy Alpert Florin, Corie Adjmi, Laura van den Berg, and Céline Keating. Marion Mell, Michael Mell, Kate Dayton, and, as ever, Laura Lyons.

ABOUT THE AUTHOR

photo credit: John Bessler

Sue Mell's story collection, *A New Day*, was a finalist for the 2021 St. Lawrence Book Award. Her debut novel, *Provenance*, won the Madville Publishing 2022 Blue Novel Award, and was selected as a Great Group Read by the Women's National Book Association, and an Indie Fiction Pick by the Community of Literary Magazines and Presses. Her collection of short essays, *Giving Care*, won the 2022 Chestnut Review Prose Chapbook Prize. Other work has appeared in *Narrative Magazine*, *Cleaver Magazine*, *Hippocampus Magazine*, *Jellyfish Review*, and elsewhere. She earned her MFA from Warren Wilson, was a 2020 BookEnds fellow at SUNY Stony Brook, and lives in Queens, New York, where she cares for her aging mom and a gray tuxedo cat named Poppy.